Milk, Cookies, and Murder
Whispering Lake Book 2
Misty Spellman

Platinum Feather Publishing

Copyright ©December 2024 by Misty Spellman

This book is a work of fiction. Names, characters, places and incidents are either the product of the author's imagination or are used fictitiously. Any resemblance to actual persons, living or dead, or to actual events or locales is entirely coincidental.

This book in its entirety and in portions is the sole property of Misty Spellman.

Milk, Cookies, and Murder Copyright ©2024 by Misty Spellman. All rights reserved, including the right to reproduce this book, or portions thereof, in any form. No part of this text may be reproduced, transmitted, downloaded, decompiled, reverse engineered, or stored in or introduced into any information storage and retrieval system, in any form or by any means, whether electronic, paperback or mechanical without the express permission of the author. The scanning, uploading and distribution of this book via the internet or via any other means without the permission of the author is illegal and punishable by law. Please purchase only authorized electronic editions and do not participate in or encourage electronic piracy of copyrighted materials.

This eBook/Paperback is licensed for your personal enjoyment only. The unauthorized reproduction or distribution of this copyrighted work is illegal. Criminal copyright infringement, including infringement without monetary gain, is investigated by the FBI and is punishable by up to 5 years in federal prison and a fine of $250,000.

Contents

1. Chapter 1 — 1
2. Chapter 2 — 8
3. Chapter 3 — 18
4. Chapter 4 — 25
5. Chapter 5 — 39
6. Chapter 6 — 48
7. Chapter 7 — 59
8. Chapter 8 — 71
9. Chapter 9 — 87
10. Chapter 10 — 102
11. Chapter 11 — 112
12. Chapter 12 — 118
13. Chapter 13 — 128
14. Chapter 14 — 137
15. Chapter 15 — 145
16. Chapter 16 — 158
17. Chapter 17 — 163
18. Chapter 18 — 172

19. Chapter 19	180
20. Chapter 20	184
Chapter	188
Chapter	189

Chapter 1

"Snow, snow, snow. Why is there so much snow?"

"Madeleine you're living in the wrong place if you want palm trees and green grass at Christmas time." I grinned and reached my mittened hand out to catch some of the crystal flakes that sparkled and reflected the glorious colors shining from a myriad of Christmas lights against the pitch black backdrop of the evening.

Snow dusted the roofs and awnings of the shops that lined the street, garlands intermixed with fairy lights wrapped around lampposts and every shop showed their pride in the intricate and unique presentations of Christmas. All had windows filled with elaborate displays and ornaments, and sported brilliant lights that twinkled cheerily. Some had candy canes as large as the children that frequented their shops out front, the white and red lights wrapped around giving them an extra shout of joy. Others had the nativity out front and one even had a blown up snowman and Rudolph on the roof. How they managed to get the city council's approval for that, I wasn't sure. Or maybe they just didn't care about the rules, in which case, more power to them.

"If you're going to judge me you might as well help me with these packages."

I grabbed a couple of the packages stacked on top of the others, balanced precariously in Madeleine's arms. I loved Christmas and all its trappings, but even I hadn't done this much shopping yet.

"Do you recycle your Christmas ornaments every year? Getting new ones and giving away the old?" I adjusted my grip on the packages.

Madeleine gave me a look. "If only it were that simple. Every year we buy more new Christmas decorations, but we never get rid of any. There's a reason our attic is stacked with boxes labeled *Christmas*."

I couldn't judge her, I did the same thing with fall decor.

A figure trod down the shoveled sidewalk, hunched against the cold.

"Ghost peppers Cammie, answer your cell phone." Ro griped as she walked up to us.

"I forgot it at home. I hate that thing." I didn't live in a small town to be on and busy twenty-four seven like city people were. "Besides," I hid a smile from her, "Madeleine has hers if you really needed us."

Ro ignored my pointed remark. "Lucy is in a state, you should come down to the café. Plus they're doing a buy one get one fifty percent off for hot chocolate."

"What's wrong with Lucy?" I hurried after her.

"What did you say to make her upset?" Madeleine demanded.

Madeleine and I fell into step on either side of Ro, looking at her expectantly.

"She's distraught and I'm very uncomfortable with tears."

"Oh." I dropped my gaze to the snow, sadness overtaking me at what she'd gone through. "She's still grieving."

"It's been six months." Ro grumbled.

"That man, who shall not be named, shattered her heart. The worthless bucket of pond scum." Madeliene growled.

My heart ached for her, she was the last person to deserve that.

"Stop walking so fast." Madeleine huffed.

"If you weren't so weighed down by consumerism you'd be able to keep up." Despite her words Ro reached over and took a large package from Madeleine.

We hurried into the café and to the table where Lucy was sitting, her face turned toward the wall. Likely to hide tears. I sat next to her and put my arm around her.

"Hi beautiful, what's going on?"

"Oh," she sniffed, "I just feel so worthless sometimes."

"Ghost pepper seeds." Ro snapped. "How dare you let anyone make you feel like that?"

Madeleine glared at her before turning a compassionate gaze to Lucy and reaching over to grab her hand. "What Ro means is that you are not the worthless one. His actions prove without a doubt that he is the worthless one. And he's most definitely going to hell."

I rubbed her back as Ro pushed some tissue paper into her hand. "Here, you're starting to look like a tomato."

"Ro!" Madeleine and I shouted.

I looked around self-consciously and noticed a few glances. Oops.

Lucy giggled, of all things. "You're the best, Ro. Thanks."

I turned my surprised gaze to Madeleine who widened her eyes at me. Why did Ro get the thanks? We were being supportive too, and we were being nice about it.

"You need something to distract you." I said. We'd all been trying to help her stay busy and not dwell on her cheating ex these last six months, but eventually she would have to fully accept it instead of avoiding it and move forward. Easier said than done.

She sighed sadly, "I thought I'd have my family for the holidays, but both of my sisters are spending Christmas with their in-laws and my parents along with some aunts and uncles and all their kids are going on a cruise."

"Ugh, who would want to be stuck with their partner in a tiny space over Christmas?" Madeleine made a face.

"People who like their partners." Ro quipped.

"I like Lawrence just fine and that is because we have space to be away from each other."

"Why don't you go with your parents on that cruise?" I didn't pay any attention to the other two.

She twisted her lips in a little grimace. "I really, really hate cruise ships."

"That's fair, can't stand them myself." Ro agreed.

"Cheer up, Lucy, you have us." Madeleine squeezed her hand.

"Not that it's saying much, but we're better than nothing." Ro was on a roll today. But still, she made Lucy giggle. I wondered if that was her goal, or just the result of her fearlessly blunt words.

I wrung my hands, I hated that anyone was sad during the weeks leading up to such a beautiful holiday. "You guys, it's Christmastime. Let's watch Christmas movies and bake cookies at my place Sunday."

"That would be nice!" Lucy's face lit up.

Ro left the table. Well, okay then.

"What kind of cookies so I know what ingredients to get?"

The ladies leaned in.

"Snickerdoodle!" Lucy bounced a little in her seat.

I smiled at her excitement, it was contagious. That, and I didn't need an excuse to be cheerful this time of year. From making hot cocoa bombs to decorating the tree and house and yard, to baking all sorts of delightful goodies, I loved it all. It was a time to spend with loved ones, curled up in snowflake and poinsettia covered fluffy blankets around a fire, watching old Christmas movies.

"I like cranberry and orange shortbread and spitzbuben."

I blinked. "We know you have fancy tastes Madeleine but what is *spitzbuben*?"

"It's a beautiful and delicious German Christmas cookie."

"Okay, let me rephrase. What the heck are you talking about?"

She looked like she was a saint surrounded by lowly peons as she took a deep breath and shook her head, gaze to the ceiling. "It's a, well it's a German Christmas dessert. It's…it's got powder sugar that dusts it and is filled with a jam."

I narrowed my eyes, "despite all your bluster, you've never made them before and don't really know exactly what they are, do you?"

She sat up indignantly, "I've tried them and I know what goes in them, that's enough."

"Looks like I missed a fun conversation." Ro appeared then with a tray that had mugs filled with a dark liquid with puffs of fluffy whipped cream covered with red and green sprinkles on top.

We were all immediately distracted by the sweet scent of chocolate.

"Mmm, this is the best hot cocoa out there." I said. "Thank you, Ro."

She may not be one for emotions or sweet words, but Ro always showed us her love through actions.

We were occupied for a couple of minutes with the delicious drink.

"Madeleine, are you visiting family for Christmas?" I asked.

"Wait, isn't it there turn to visit you?" Lucy frowned.

"I'm glad at least someone is invested in my life." Madeleine took a sip of her drink while I sputtered. "Anyway, they're coming to stay with us." She pressed her lips together and quickly changed the subject. "Ro, are you going to Cammie's tomorrow for the cookie making?"

Ro looked over at me, "that depends on what Christmas music will be playing."

I smiled. "That's easy, I'm playing movies, not music."

"Fine. As long as it's not Barbie and the Nutcracker."

"Oh I loved that one when I was little." Lucy said.

"I don't have that one, no worries. What cookies do you want to make?"

"I'd rather watch you three make them and then I get to eat them."

"What a user." Madeleine smiled into her mug, taking the sting out of the words.

"Is Gavin driving down for any part of the holidays?" Lucy asked eagerly. She and my little cousin had struck up a sweet friendship during his many visits.

"He'll be here for the parade next weekend."

"He's lovely."

I stared at Ro. "Did you just call another human *lovely*?" It was a Christmas miracle.

"Don't get used to it."

Lucy looked up as two people passed by the table. "Charles and Jenny!" She exclaimed. With a smile she got up and hugged the youth.

"You're looking lovely as usual." The man, Charles, said in a fatherly way.

Lucy smiled brightly, "thank you. Are you ready for Christmas?"

Jenny looked at her dad with a little smile, "dad's been working so much we haven't fully decorated yet. We always decorate the tree together."

Charles looked self-conscious. Maybe he felt bad for working so many long hours.

"That's very special."

"We'll get to it soon." Charles promised his daughter. "In the meantime, we're going to make hot cocoa bombs tonight."

She bounced a little at that, a sweet smile on her round face. She must have been in her early teens but she still hadn't gotten rid of all her baby fat. I hadn't either at that age to the chagrin of my mother and the delight of the school bullies.

They chatted for a few more minutes then said goodbye and Lucy sat back down.

"I used to babysit her. Charles' is a single dad and when she was little they lived across the street."

"She's a cutie." I went to take a sip but found I was staring into an empty mug. How disappointing.

"She was a beautiful baby, too. But I doubt she'd appreciate you calling her a cutie at her age. Kids these days want to be called," Lucy made air quotes, "sexy."

"Individuals with raging hormones and a still not fully developed brain should not be allowed to be called sexy." Ro said.

I hummed my agreement even as I made a grocery list on my small notepad. I would need a lot more flour and butter. And apparently jam.

Chapter 2

We didn't have book club during the busy holidays so Saturday morning I got ready to go grocery shopping and then start the two hour drive to Chesterton, the city where my family all lived and were having a whole family get together. I was strangely excited about it.

"It must be the holiday spirit." I told Rutherford as he sat on my nightstand watching me with those big green eyes. "Don't look at me so balefully, you've already been fed." My cat had managed to con all of his babysitters over the years into giving him extra meals. Somehow he managed to never lose the weight he gained during those times.

I shooed him off the nightstand and smoothed my bed covers. Christmas came around only once a year and I planned to celebrate it to the full. That included changing out my entire bedspread to one with a woven-jacquard design that had holiday bells, poinsettia flowers, berries, and swirls tastefully decorating it. The shams also had bells, holly leaves and berries. Gavin had gotten the set for me one year and I hadn't changed it out since. Besides, it only came out once a year and I thought it was beautiful as if it were brand new every year.

I bustled out into the living room, fluffing the tree as I went by it. It wasn't decorated yet, I was waiting for Gavin to come down and do it with me. We'd started that tradition when he lived with me while he was going to college. A light, musky scent of balsam fir, along with juniper and a hint of citrus tickled my senses and I breathed deeply. It wasn't that I had a real tree—really, who could see me wandering through the woods looking for a tree to cut down and drag back to irreverently strap on top of my perfect little yellow bug?—no, it was a spray I used, and it held all the warmth and sweetness of Christmas in a bottle.

I could bask in the scent later, right now it was time to go grocery shopping so I had ingredients for cookies.

As I left I glanced back at my little cottage one more time, making sure everything was as it should be. Lights along the eves that my handyman had put up, a wreath with magnolia leaves, succulents, moss, pinecones, and groups of red berries hung on my door, a little family of light up deer behind the picket fence in my petite yard. I loved it.

My VW bug groaned as I turned the key, then rumbled to life. "Good job Buttercup." I kept it plugged into an outlet so the battery stayed warm and I didn't come out to a car that wouldn't start because of the cold. That had happened a few times. Already I'd driven Lucy to work due to colder than usual nights leaking her battery.

As the keeper of the town's historical archives and the person who arranged the Cultural Arts Center displays, I like to believe that I am deliberate, thoughtful, and organized. That belief is shattered every time I go to the grocery store. Each aisle I stroll down hides something from me so I need to go back another time.

The second time down the produce aisle I stopped to look at the squash and noticed Victor Tjernagel, resident hermit, picking out tomatoes. He must have been shy because he rarely spoke to people and always had a dour look on his face.

I smiled cheerily, "hi Mr. Tjernagel. Merry Christmas! Have you set up a tree in your cabin?"

He aimed unfriendly blue eyes partly obscured under bushy grey eyebrows my way. "Not everyone likes this cursed holiday. Mind your own business, lady." He spit out and stomped past me. Well, more like did the stiff old man walk past me. I was too surprised to say anything else.

I tried to shake off his angry words and finished my shopping. Ro would say I was too sensitive, but I felt bad that what I'd said upset him so much.

Groceries in hand I drove home and put everything away. That task done I checked my phone. Not my home phone that I preferred using, but the handheld device that was a source of both annoyance and sometimes help, such as when I was pushed down a flight of stairs and an ambulance needed to be called. A little number three showed that I had some texts from Gavin.

Gavin: *Hey! Excited to see U at the family thing today. Drive safe!*

Gavin: *I know UR not big on texting but U R coming, right?*

Gavin: *U better not leave me alone with those people Cammie Lynn Lockett.*

I laughed a little and typed back. *Sorry, I was at the store. I'll be there probably right after it kicks off, I'm leaving now.*

As soon as I got back into the car my phone, which I was still holding, did a little jig, vibrating in my hand and scaring the daylights out of me. I dropped it onto the other seat like it was burning hot.

With an embarrassed look around to make sure no one had seen that—there was no one else out on my street—I picked it up and checked the texts.

Gavin: *Thank goodness!!!*

I started driving. The cottages lining the street looked like pastel gumdrops with white icing frosting the eves in the form of glittering snow. It was a lovely sight and once again I was happy I'd moved away from the city.

A little over two hours later I arrived at my aunt's two story behemoth of a house. It was beautiful, situated in a gated neighborhood, and had a pristine, manicured lawn. I disliked it intensely. My stomach always started shifting uncomfortably when I arrived there. I took a breath. It would be fine, I was going to see people I loved. And hopefully we'd all have wonderful conversations over spiked hot cocoa. It was Christmastime after all. And with the amount of money they'd probably spent to have their house professionally decorated outside and inside it would be so wasteful to not enjoy it to the full.

Per usual I was the last one at the house and when I knocked on the door I was welcomed into a boisterous crowd. One of my cousin's kids, Abel, raced around with a plane, screaming out the sounds he probably thought a plane made. A whole airport would be quieter than him. The teens were lounging in the game room, two were playing a video game on the TV, three were on their phones.

"Come on in, Cammie. We were worried you weren't going to come." The oldest cousin in the family, Jason was the one who owned the house with his lovely model wife who thought eating more than a cup of popcorn for lunch was the reason our society had so many back problems. I thought it might be because everyone sat hunched over a computer these days, but what did I know.

"How are you?" We hugged.

"Great! We're taking a trip to Hawaii for January and February because the cold bothers Poppi so much."

"That will be fun." I ignored the slight bragging in his tone. If he could afford to live in Hawaii for a couple of months, good for him.

He opened the coat closet for me to hang my coat up. I stuffed it in next to all the others. Shouldn't a house this big have a decent sized coat closet?

"Cammie!" My mother's commanding voice rose over the din of people talking and kids yelling as they played together.

I waved and stepped into the house, toward her. Inside I stopped in my tracks, taking it all in. It looked like Santa's Christmas factory exploded. I loved Christmas more than most people but why was a real sleigh hanging from the twenty-foot ceiling?

I hurried over to my mom, giving a friendly pat on the back of my cousin Joan as I passed. She was gesturing widely as she told some story to a couple of other family members and paused to wave at me.

"Hi, mom." Mom and I hugged and she backed up, hands still on my arms as she looked me over. "What are you wearing?"

I looked down. "I'm pretty sure the description on the website said this is a cable knit sweater. And those are jeans."

She pursed her lips but didn't comment. I had thought I looked fine but now I glanced at other people to see what they were wearing.

"We know who has the fashion sense of the family." Gavin popped up next to me. He was wearing a brightly printed scarf, a white sweater over a purple turtleneck and skinny pants hitting his ankles above loafers.

"Not you, given that ridiculous getup." My mother shot back. Her sister, Gavin's mom, joined us.

"Come on Jane, I think it's kind of fun." My aunt said before smiling a greeting at me. "Hi Cammie, it's nice of you to finally join us. It's wonderful to have all of our family here."

"I'm happy to see you, Lana."

"What have you been investing your time in these days?" From her soft, high-pitched voice to her perfectly manicured nails, Lana was the picture of elegance. Gavin took after her a great deal.

I opened my mouth but closed it again. I couldn't tell her about the drama that had unfolded a few months ago, my mom would probably faint if I went around telling the family how I found a pile of bones belonging to a man who'd been murdered thirty years earlier.

"We recently hired a new city manager so she's been supporting me in expanding the historical archives and displays a bit." It was lame to anyone who didn't appreciate the simplicity of my life. So, virtually everyone.

"You're too modest." Gavin swished the fancy margarita he was holding. "Cammie solved a murder not that long ago."

Oh no.

"Yes, I did hear about that." Lana said, glancing at mom.

My mother tsked disapprovingly. "We encourage you to get out of your bubble and meet some nice men and you go and fall into a murder investigation."

"We all have our gifts." I needed to shift the conversation to something else. "Lana, I never got to congratulate you on your upcoming grandchild."

My mom widened her eyes at me, "you make it sound like it's a movie being released soon, not a new baby is coming into the family."

"We all knew what she meant." Gavin had stepped away to say something to someone else but he turned back to us now. "Not all of us are in tune with baby terminology."

"Unfortunately. Goodness knows I'll never get a grandchild from you." Lana's lips turned down at the corners as she gazed at Gavin with that disappointed expression she and my mom had perfected and weaponized. I'd never met grandma Frida, but I could imagine that she was the one who taught them the look.

I needed to separate Lana and Gavin. Now. Before my mother could join and point fingers at me, her ungrateful only child.

"Gavin, did you see that platter over there? I have no idea what's on it. It looks interesting but I'd rather you take a bite first since you're so adventurous with food and I like to play it safe. Mom, Lana, it's so nice to see you both, let's chat later." I looped arms with Gavin and guided him toward the tables draped in blood red tablecloths and embroidered with swirling gold. "So ostentatious." I muttered under my breath.

Gavin leaned toward me, "I like my finery and all but Jason and Poppi are over the top."

"I guess if it brings them joy then more power to them."

A couple of my cousin's little kids were looking our way. I waved and they smiled shyly and waved back. They were cuties. Noisy, but cute.

Gavin bravely sampled some of the finger food for me, assuring me that there were no allergens that would blow my face up or some horrible thing I didn't want to eat in them. Joan came over to us and we hugged.

"I've been so busy with the art gallery I haven't had a chance to come visit you." She said.

I would have made a comment about her being welcome to come to my place whenever she had time but she'd been saying the same thing for the past six years, so instead I changed the subject.

"I heard that you might be getting engaged, is the lucky guy here?" it seemed like a safe enough thing to ask.

She smiled dreamily. "He's wonderful. Distinguished, wealthy." she wiggled her eyebrows at me, "and very knowledgeable of the arts."

I didn't comment that I thought a person fell in love with their partner's character and the way they laughed and their sense of humor, not how distinguished they were. But what did I know, I was the family old maid.

"And you, you haven't dated for a long time, as far as I know. You must be excited."

Worry started to gnaw at my gut and I focused on her, "why would I be excited?"

"About the guy your mom found for you."

My eyes nearly rolled back in my head even as I could feel my blood pressure shooting through the roof. After this many decades of life how was she still throwing men at me and expecting me to put up with them like I was in my twenties or thirties? I was set in my ways and fine with it.

"I'm not sure about any of that." *Change the subject, change the subject.* "Have you read anything good lately? I've I found some delightful historical mysteries that I have been binging." When we were younger Joan and I were the two the people of the family who enjoyed reading the most, so I thought it was a safe topic.

"That sounds fun, I'm just too busy with work and Gerald has been taking us on so many vacations that I haven't had time to get into anything lately. You understand."

Most of what I did on vacation was read so no, I couldn't understand. But I nodded anyway.

Music crooned through the overhead speakers, I spoke with an aunt and then had an interesting conversation with one of the teenagers—interesting meaning I couldn't understand about a third of the language used—and an hour later I found myself talking to mother and my uncle Hendry while nibbling on a cupcake that was covered in a dark green frosting Christmas tree with pearls and sprinkles making up the decorations.

The loud voice of Gavins sister, Chelsey, caught my attention.

"You know that's a foolish thing to do. Why would you even consider that?" She was pointing her finger right in Gavin's face. He looked utterly put out. Even I knew pointing at someone put them on edge. Not even my cat liked being pointed at.

"Because it brings me joy." He shot back, not backing down.

"You won't be giving mom and dad any grandchildren, you go into a profession that you really can't grow and get acclaim in, and now you want to host these crazy parties?"

"They're not crazy!" He sounded like he was working to contain his exasperation. "You make them sound like they're strip club parties. They're rooftop garden parties that my salon and the neighboring tattoo studio are sponsoring. I like getting to know new people and it gives me a chance to network."

"Gavin, are you sure that's wise? A lot of people will be there and you don't know if they're of good social standing." Lana added.

His shoulders drooped forward subtly, enough that I saw only because I was paying close attention to him. "Mom, the people I work with and employ and have as friends aren't unsavory people. They're just like you and I."

"You should listen to your family Gavin, clearly you're in the wrong here." Poppi butted in.

My blood started to heat, why was she getting involved now? If everyone went back to what they were doing and ignored the immediate family squabble those three would go to their separate corners and everything would smooth out.

"You're a foot model, what do you know?" Gavin shot back.

I closed my eyes as if it would stop the trainwreck in front of me from happening.

"Oh!" She let out a high-pitched gasp.

"Gavin!" Jason's mom put her arm around her daughter-in-law as she teared up, whimpering.

"That was inappropriate." One of our cousins scolded.

"Oh for heavens sakes, she's not even crying for real." I knew I shouldn't say anything, I really did, but it just flooded out. The whole thing was absurd. Just because he had a different viewpoint didn't mean he needed to be attacked by *everyone*.

"Cammie!" My mother snapped.

I glanced at her, my cheeks heating in embarrassment. Still, I wouldn't leave Gavin alone. If it was just his sister and mom then fine, but if others were going to get involved I would defend him. He deserved to have at least one person on his side.

"Cammie, stay out of this." Jason's tone held a warning.

Stay out of...what about Poppi?

I felt like a robot, staring out at them, my body rigid. I turned stiffly to Gavin who was standing up now, glaring at Jason.

"I think it's best if I leave before I speak the truth and more people get riled up." My voice cracked.

"I'm coming too, there's a delightful new boutique restaurant I want to show you. They have wonderful dessert." Gavin talked as though not every single person in the room was staring at us and hooked his arm through mine.

I made it out the door without bursting into tears.

Chapter 3

Afternoon the next day rolled around and I couldn't be more excited to have the ladies at my house. After dealing with my family I needed people around who gave me peace. It was still frustrating to think about, couldn't everyone just get along for one whole evening? It was Christmas, shouldn't people be more charitable this time of year?

Pushing the hollow pain I felt whenever a fight broke out like that into an emotional storage bin I opened the door as soon as I heard snow crunch under tires. Madeliene had driven both Lucy and Ro in her SUV. I stared at it and a grin took over my face. Her SUV had reindeer antlers on top and eyelashes on the headlights. They must have forced Ro into a car that was decorated like that kicking and screaming.

I left the door open so they could come in unhindered and once again fussed over the ingredients I had spread out on my counter.

"How many cookies are you planning on making?" Ro widened her eyes at the ingredients, the bowls, and all the trays I'd put out.

"Oh this is wonderful! You're always such a gracious host." Lucy came in carrying a bowl of her own filled with measuring cups, the one thing I didn't have extra of.

The ladies hung their coats in the coat closet and left their winter boots by the door, stuffing their feet into the slippers I provided. This time of year everyone who came to my house should have a comfy pair of slippers.

I glanced at Ro and couldn't help the chuckle that escaped.

She crossed her arms and tilted her head, her lips twitching as if she wanted to break into a smile but was holding it back, "and what's so funny?"

"Never in my life did I think I would see you in a pair of adorable penguin slippers. This moment is priceless."

Lucy looked over at her and giggled. Even Madeleine looked amused.

"You should think about putting on an elf costume and joining the parade next weekend." Madeleine's eyes lit with good humor, "if they're still looking, you could even be Mrs. Claus."

"I'm flattered, but wouldn't the part of a white haired lady who wears outlandish clothes and talks to elves be best suited for someone like yourself?"

"As a matter of fact, I turned down the role." Madeleine seemed to take it as a point of pride instead of an insult.

"Ro, you never told me what you wanted to make, were you serious about sitting on the sidelines?" I opened a cabinet and reached inside.

"Yes, I much prefer to chat with you while you do all the labor." Her eyes crinkled.

I smiled widely, "that's too bad, because while you may not be making cookies, I got this just for you." I produced a gingerbread house kit.

The humor on Ro's face dropped like a stone while Madeleine and Lucy laughed.

"And you have to make it as beautiful as possible since I'll be displaying it in my window."

Ro said something under her breath that may have been *Christmas tyrant*.

"Okay then, let's get started," I smiled "I even got everything for the ridiculously fancy sounding cookies you wanted Madeleine, they're over on this side." I gestured.

Forty minutes later Lucy was fussing at the counter.

"What's wrong?" I wiggled in next to her at the crowded counter. I'd been working at the island with Ro.

"I think there's a little hole in this flour bag but I can't figure out where. It just leaves these little tufts on the counter whenever I move it and it's driving me mad."

"Hmm," I lifted the bag with both hands.

Fwoosh.

Lucy's hands flew to her face and her eyes got wide right before Madeleine and Ro burst into gales of laughter.

Try to breathe through the coating of flour, don't panic, feel your way to the sink.

Madeleine put a plastic bag around what was left of the flour bag and Lucy guided me to the sink where I tilted my face down and proceeded to sneeze the flour off my face. I pried my watering eyes open and grabbed paper towels, wetting them and wiping the flour off my face.

Lucy stood next to me, trying to hold in her giggling and failing miserably.

"Lucy Marie Dewley, did you do that on purpose?" I knew she hadn't but I had to at least pretend I hadn't just stupidly slapped myself in the face with a fistful of flour because I was too hairbrained to put a plastic bag around it instead of looking for the hole. Which, by the way, I had thought was a little pinprick. It was not.

"No of course not!" Her laughter wasn't convincing.

Two hours later we'd laughed, paused to watch the first half of It's A Wonderful Life, burned a pan of cookies while we were watching said movie, and had each eaten far too many.

"Mmm, I think my new favorite is the cranberry and orange shortbread cookies Madeleine so kindly suggested." I nibbled on another one.

Ro nodded, "they were quite good." As the resident healthy person of the group, Ro was usually the one with a salad and muffins that contained raisins. This Christmas though she was surprisingly open to eating like the rest of us sugar craved mortals.

"You said you were taking some time off this week, doing anything in particular?" Madeleine leaned back on the couch she shared with Lucy.

I swallowed a bite of cookie I'd taken and started coughing, grabbing my mug of hot cocoa and clearing my throat with it.

"No need to be so dramatic, it's not like I asked if you had a secret boyfriend."

Ro's eyes lit up like a shark sensing blood. Oh no, Madeleine had just made me a target. "Christmas romance? Did this just turn into a hallmark movie?"

"I love those!" Lucy said.

Ro gave her a disgusted look, "don't even." She turned her gaze back to me, "if you say yes know that I will judge you."

"Ghost Peppers you all will be the death of me. To answer your question," I quickly changed the subject, "I will be volunteering at both the animal shelter's craft fair where they raise money using the booths people purchase to sell their homemade goods, and at the toy drive for children in the city who might not have as much."

"With all those good things you're doing you've certainly made me feel like Scrooge. Any chance they need more help?"

I grinned at Ro, "we could always use more volunteers."

"Tell me when and where."

"I will. Oh!" I lifted a finger, "I have something interesting to show you all." I got up and hustled into my bedroom, going to the closet where on a shelf I had placed a very special find that I had discovered in the recesses of the Cultural Arts Center archive room when I was doing a deep cleaning. I had wrapped it in a soft cloth to protect it. I now pulled it off the shelf, delicately wrapping my arms around it like it was a baby. I didn't know why exactly but it felt precious to me.

Everyone was watching me with rapt attention as I walked back and placed it on the coffee table in front of them. Carefully I unwrapped the cloth to reveal the box.

"Oh." Madeleine breathed. I was glad I wasn't the only one who had that strange feeling about it.

Lucy reached towards it and stopped just before touching it, the pads of her fingers hovering over it.

Ro leaned forward in her chair, studying it. "I don't understand, what is it about this box?"

I turned it so they could see it from all angles, the painstaking carvings, the pure beautiful wood that had been stained a great many years ago and still held a luster.

"This is the best part." I popped the latch using the cloth, not touching it directly with my hands, and lifted the lid.

It felt like everyone was collectively holding their breath.

Once the curved top of the box was fully up the music box inside with all it's strings, also crafted with the precision of a master, began to move as music gently played, haunting and beautiful all at once.

Lucy had wrapped her arms around herself. Everyone looked as shocked as I had felt when I'd first seen it. Even now it raised goosebumps on my arms.

"Tell me it's just because we're fans of history that we feel so drawn toward it and not something weird." Ro said warily.

"I assume so, I felt like I was calling to me the first time I saw it on the shelf."

"Where did you find this?" Lucy was studying the scrollwork that had been carefully hand etched into the wood.

"It was hidden in the corner on the top shelf of one of the units in the very back of the archives." I was surprised I had never found it before when I'd been cleaning back there.

"There's just something about it." Madeleine was frowning, "Clearly this exquisite work was done by a very knowledgeable wood carver."

"What kind of wood is this?" Lucy asked.

"I thought it looked like cherry." I said.

"Or Swiss pear." Row leaned forward thoughtfully, "it would have been harder to get and more exotic back when this was likely carved."

"Are there any initials on it? Something like this would be a family heirloom, I'm sure they'd want it back." Madeleine lifted it with the cloth, looking at the bottom and the sides carefully.

"I tried that. I couldn't see anything but maybe your eyes are sharper than mine."

"Hardly." still, she peered at it.

"I guess it's a Christmas mystery." Ro said.

"Isn't there just something about it that makes you want to get it back to its rightful owner?" Lucy asked.

"I told my therapist about you and she says you're an empath." Madeleine said

Ro leaned forward with a troublemaking grin on her face, "what does she say about me?"

Madeleine tilted her nose in the air and gave her a dismissing glance, "I don't bother mentioning you."

Ro laughed.

"Are you all going to that ornament making class at the library this weekend?" Madeleine asked.

"I'm working so I'll have to be there." Ro took a sip of her green tea, which she claimed would help even out the sugar a little.

I nodded, "I'll be there. So will Gavin." He was coming down early and we figured it would be a fun project before the parade.

"I was thinking about going but I have to—" Lucy paused, her face becoming slightly nervous then she quickly changed the subject, "look at your cat."

Rutherford was stretched up on his hind legs, reaching toward the lowest ornament I had on the tree, which was quite high given the fact that I had a cat.

"Rutherford!" I clapped my hands loudly.

You would think that he would have the decency to at least act startled. He lazily turned his head to look at me, green eyes curious and mischievous, and he reached his paw up one more time as he looked at me, batting at the ornament.

I got up and marched over to him. "Bad kitty." I scooped him into my arms and carried him back to the couch.

Ro was smiling and she winked at the cat, "that's the way to train her.

"I think it's time to finish that Christmas movie since we only got halfway through, are you up for it?" Madeleine asked.

I agreed enthusiastically.

"I can't believe you haven't seen this one before." Lucy said to Ro.

"What? I spent a whole lot of Christmases overseas working."

"What, they don't have Christmas movies in politically unstable countries? I feel like that's a stereotype." I grabbed the remote.

Ro gave me a disgruntled look.

The ladies left late—for us—and I finished cleaning up before going to bed. Everyone had pitched in to help put things away and get the dishes in the dishwasher and wipe down the countertops so I didn't have much left to do. They'd also each taken a gallon zip lock bag of cookies.

I gave Rutherford a cat treat and made my way down to my room. I had tomorrow off as I would be going in to the animal shelter later that morning to volunteer so I adjusted my morning alarm. I also set the hand carved music box, wrapped in its soft cloth, back on the shelf. I would be doing some research on it. What secrets could it hold?

Chapter 4

"Mr. Blake! I didn't know your wife was so talented." I picked up a block of resin that had an African baobab tree in the center and an elephant, a cheetah, and a giraffe drinking from a pool of water. The work was painstaking and exquisite. And expensive. I put the block back.

"Thank you! And please call me Anthony. She has smaller items here as well that she can describe to you better than I can, she had to run off for a moment. This is one of my favorites." he showed me a coaster and cutting board set, with beautiful pale wood covered in resin and the design of a wave washing up on shore. Simple, elegant, and beautiful. If it was within my budget I had just found a Christmas gift for my mother. I tried to be subtle as I looked at the back and front for a price sticker. He also, subtly, nudged a plaque with prices on it forward. I was relieved, it was something I could afford.

"I'll come back around to tell your wife how amazing her work is. In the meantime would you be able to take payment for these?"

"Certainly!" Ever the dutiful husband he rang me up, took payment on a little swiper connected to his phone, and packaged up the items, carefully wrapping them in fluffy white and pale blue tissue paper and putting them into a sturdy Christmas bag.

"Thank you." I said goodbye and hurried off to get back to my volunteer work.

We were in a warehouse on the edge of town that had been transformed into a Christmas craft fair paradise by us volunteers yesterday and early this morning before all the vendors came to set up. The decorations included snowflake lights, big red ribbon bows, and a large sleigh with gold runners and a plush red velvet cushion that Santa sat on with a lineup of children waiting to talk to him.

Ro had vanished when the children arrived and I had a feeling I knew where she was. I made my way past throngs of people and went to a door in the back of the glittering warehouse. Through the door and a hallway the second warehouse held the kennels and cat cages. It was no ordinary warehouse, heated and with plenty of space for the animals that had been shipped here from city rescues that were overcrowded. This place was a special sanctuary. One part of it was just for senior dogs and cats that required extra care and whose family were pond scum for leaving them in their old age because they were inconvenient.

As I suspected, Ro sat with the old dogs.

"Hiding from all the people?"

"I don't hide, I carefully extricate myself from dangerous situations and find a safehouse."

I opened my arms wide, "how are a bunch of children waiting to tell Santa their biggest dreams dangerous?"

Her lips twitched, "dangerous for them. If one more small person ran in front of me screaming I was going to start teaching a class on discipline and manners."

I laughed. To each their own. "Okay, carry on. I happen to like the happy hubbub of Christmas shopping, so I'll be out there if you need me."

"Wait, I'll go with you. I need to get some of that healthy peppermint bark before it runs out." She got up and brushed her pants off. Dog hair was unforgiving and I handed her a massive lint roller that hung outside the cage. "Thanks."

We left together and made our way to the main room. On the table next to the "healthy" peppermint bark the woman sold clearly unhealthy Christmas mix she called reindeer chow that contained chex covered in powdered sugar mixed with mini pretzels and peanut butter cups and red and green m and ms. Yum!

A loud voice at the booth next to us caught my attention and I lingered, slowly looking over all the food the woman offered while tuning in to the conversation.

"Yeah, I sealed the deal like that." The man speaking snapped his fingers. "You should have seen his face when he found out he wasn't included." He laughed. It was a harsh, mocking laugh that made the hair on the back of my neck stand up.

Ro was frowning over at them and I couldn't help glancing that way. The man looked like a sleezy salesman. Overly greased hair, similarly greasy smile, the man—how did my cousin's kid put it at the family get together?—gave me the *ick*. I didn't need to be fluent in teenlish to know that was not a compliment.

His companion asked him something so quietly I couldn't hear.

"No, Christmas is just a marketing scheme and that parade is for children and people who don't want to grow up. The whole thing is for chumps."

Anthony Blake had been striding down this way but when he saw the two men he faltered. He must have heard what they were saying because his face flushed a deep shade of pink and anger burned in his eyes. He continued forward with determination, walking up to them.

"What a surprise to see you here, Darwin. This is a family event, lowlife scum shouldn't be here."

I may have been trying to pretend I wasn't paying attention before but now I was raptly staring at the trio. The women behind the booth they were standing at looked uncomfortable.

"Careful Blake, you might make people think we're friends." The man laughed.

"That's an interesting thought, do sociopaths have friends?"

My jaw nearly hit the floor. I glanced at Ro and she looked like she could use a bag of popcorn as she watched the exchange with bright interest.

"Now now, such a bitter man."

"Anthony." A woman hurried up to the attorney. She was beautiful with chocolate brown hair that waved gracefully to her shoulders and intelligent brown eyes behind blue grey framed glasses. Mrs. Blake. "I could use your help with a sale." She spared Darwin a quick glance of barely contained contempt before grabbing Anthony's hand and pulling him away.

Things settled down when Anthony Blake and his wife left and the sinister duo were on their way in the opposite direction.

"I am very glad I decided to come get that peppermint bark." Ro said.

"You look like you enjoyed that." My heart was racing. Confrontations like that gave me hives. Hmm, maybe that was it. Up until that thought I'd assumed I was just allergic to my family.

"Mr. Blake's s comeback was inspiring."

"Oh goodness." I shook my head. I wouldn't admit it but I would very much like to know what had happened between Anthony and Darwin that bred such animosity.

My cell phone listed a missed call from Gavin so when I got home I took my home phone from the stand and sat on the couch with Rutherford, dialing Gavin back. He was a night owl so a nine pm call wasn't going to upset him.

"Hello!" he greeted, far too exuberant for the time of night.

"Sorry I missed your call, I was volunteering at an event for the animal shelter. What's going on?"

"That's lovely. I'm volunteering for an animal shelter this year as well, they're hosting a Christmas gala."

Of course, his volunteering would involve him getting dressed up in a suit. He probably was helping to plan and execute the whole thing so it was done right. I smiled. "I want pictures."

"That's a given darling."

I paused, waiting for him to answer my initial question, knowing how much he hated gaps in conversation.

Something akin to a huff sounded on the other end. "There's another family thing with just my immediate family coming up and I don't want to attend but if I don't that will potentially make it worse than if I do."

It was almost easier when the whole family, extended relatives and all, were in attendance than when there was no one else to speak with except the people you were usually irritated with. Unless of course the whole family got involved in the argument and ganged up on said person.

"Given the time of year there should be extra good will. I know you and your family want to enjoy the time together, especially now with these changes coming up for your sister. I think that if you didn't go you'd feel bad." He was more sensitive than he let on. "Plus, if you don't go it's automatically your fault for not trying to be a cooperative member of the family. If you do and someone else starts the fight—which usually happens—then you can at least feel better about yourself walking away." I paused, thinking about something I'd heard from a therapist online. "If their toxicity is too much you need to distance yourself, even cutting ties. There is no shame in taking care of your own soul." Which would mean cutting ties with everyone in the family because they were all close. Like a pack of wolves. Except me, that was a given. I'd pick Gavin over everyone else any day. Not that I would ever repeat that to any of my family, and it would be horribly sad if it came to that.

"That won't be necessary, and I think you're right, I should go." He sounded less jovial than usual and it created a sad pit in my stomach.

"Don't forget that you're coming for the parade this weekend."

"How could I ever forget! I'm going to drag you through all the shops at least once, probably twice. I need to still get gifts for some of my employees." He had perked up again. "And I need to bother Lucy. She seemed sad when she drove up for her last haircut."

"Yes, she thought her cheating ex was buying her a ring to propose and it turns out it was a gift to his other lady. Even though it's been a while she still feels inadequate."

"That scallywag. If he's at the parade I may try and shove his face down into the snow."

"He lives in the next town and I haven't seen him around since the incident."

"How'd Lucy find out?"

"It was a complete accident. She was going through his travel bag to get a breath mint while they were in the city for dinner and she came across the ring—which was a gemstone, not a diamond—with a note for a woman named Olivia."

"Oh no." He breathed.

"It was devastating. She ran out of there before he came back from the restroom and called me. I drove to the city and picked her up so she wouldn't have to ride with him." It had been a tearful two hour ride back to town. There was something that my mind snagged on, but I wasn't sure why. "She seems like she's been keeping a secret of her own for the last couple of weeks, so I wonder if she found someone else to date or if she is emotionally hiding."

"Not likely, she has the same emotional energy as I do. You've had my head on your shoulder during many a breakup."

I'd been the older cousin he'd always gone to when distraught. His parents loved him, even if they did always back his sister in arguments, but they weren't able to validate his emotions. That part of the family, my mom and her three sisters and grandma, were logical, math driven people who thought tough love was needed in every situation, even when all a person wanted was just to be heard and shown support and compassion. The brothers were only slightly less demanding.

"You're right. She's probably just going through the stages of grief right now. Anyway, she said she's excited to see you."

"It's going to be a party weekend." He said cheerily.

I laughed, "you can make a complete mess of my house as long as you use Christmas decorations."

"That's a promise!"

We got ready to hang up.

"Hey, wait. Call me when that family dinner is over, okay?" I worried he'd keep his emotions bottled up. The last time he'd done that was when he was living with me while going to college and when his emotions finally demanded to be acknowledged I had found him in tears on the bathroom floor with a very big, very full glass of Chardonnay. It had been his third if his burbling and the thirteen hours of sleep he'd had after had been any indication. Thankfully, that had been the only time he'd kept things to himself to the point where he was hurting that much.

"I promise. Thank you for loving me."

I laughed. "That's not something you thank people for." I sobered. "Your parents love you too, they're just not sure how to relate to you. Your sister is just like them so it's easier."

He sighed. "I guess. Okay, bye now."

"Bye."

He would be okay. I hadn't received a call or anything from my mom after the hubbub at the party where I was given the cold shoulder by almost everyone after defending Gavin. She would eventually come around and call me to chew me out and then invite me to another event. She still loved me, even if she disapproved of the decisions I made.

I put a historical mystery documentary on and cuddled into one of my robins egg blue plush barrel back chairs with a poinsettia stitched blanket. My eyes grew heavy. At some point Rutherford jumped into my lap and started kneading me, purring.

Drrring.

Drrring.

I blinked and sat up. My back howled at me that someone my age shouldn't dare to sleep in a chair like that and not expect my body to respond with violence.

Rutherford sat up and sneezed in my face. Apparently that was the punishment I got for waking him.

I had left the handheld home phone on the circular side table next to me and I blinked at the bleary words on the little screen, holding it closer and then farther away as I tried to get my gaze to focus. Ah, my mother. And it was six in the morning. Six in the morning! Was she in the hospital?

"Hello?" I croaked.

"Were you still sleeping? It's already six."

I rubbed my face. "Is everything okay mom?"

"Of course not. Your aunt Jennifer wants to know if you need an intervention."

My groan was contained. Barely. "I hope you told her that just because I didn't marry for money or choose some flashy job doesn't mean I'm unhappy or worthless."

She didn't say anything. Of course not, because it did mean that to them.

"I worry about you. Living out there in the boonies, never finding anyone to attach to. Your cousins are all close and get together all the time. They support one another. You should be living here too, being there for them and they can do the same. Maybe you need counseling."

It was too early for this conversation. Again.

"Mom, we've talked about this before. I'm well into midlife and I'm happy. This was my choice and just because it isn't what you'd do doesn't mean it's wrong." I'd argued before that I didn't live in the *boonies,* I lived in a perfectly respectable town, and I'd dated in my younger years and hadn't found a soulmate and didn't want to settle.

My mom went on to make her argument, one I'd heard countless times. I wondered if she had a script written by now.

I tried to change the subject to something, anything, else but she wouldn't have it.

"After Christmas I promised to introduce you to a very nice man."

My eyes drifted closed and I rubbed a hand over my face. "I appreciate that you care, but I don't have any interest in dating." I almost added, 'especially since he lives in a city two hours away,' but that would just give her more of a reason to try and bring me back to the city where she could pop by whenever she wanted.

Several more minutes of conversation that just went in circles and she finally said that she wanted me to come for the weekend. I explained that I had commitments this weekend and she finally gave up, saying it was hurtful that I wouldn't come see her, but she would talk to me when she saw me at the next family Christmas party.

After that conversation I wouldn't be going to sleep. What I needed was a coffee and a pastry. Maybe something slightly less sugary, like a piece of banana bread.

I showered, fed Rutherford, and slipped into a festive red sweater, jeans, and a pretty red patterned scarf. By the time I left the house the clock read 8:30.

Buttercup groaned and then puttered along down the road for me, faithful as ever. This early in the morning on a weekday I managed to get a good parking spot in front of my favorite place, the Sleepy Kitty Café which had the cutest logo of an adorable cartoon cat with big eyes hooded with tiredness holding a steaming cup of coffee in its paws. Now the logo sign was decorated with a Santa hat and scarf around the kitten's neck, and the mug was a special Christmas mug. Ironically the same mug that they were selling inside. The Green words on a backdrop of red said *It's either serial killer documentaries or Christmas movies. We're either sleighin or slayin'.* I thought it was quite cute, but after what had happened a few months ago, finding a pile of bones that had turned out to be a murdered victim and then solving the crime inadvertently so we could save the historical society, I didn't want to tempt fate to throw anything else into my path. Murder victims, or ghosts. That was a whole other story. I still didn't have any answers for that one.

Across the street and down the sidewalk I caught sight of a familiar caramel colored coat. Lucy. I hoped she was feeling better. She didn't like to bother people, or do anything she assumed was bothering other people, so she wasn't always the first to reach out when she needed support, emotional or otherwise. But why was she at the old antique shop? The owner had decided to retire and was leaving the space. It hadn't even been posted on the market for rent but Lucy and—was that Mandy the realtor?—had gone inside and were now coming back out. Mandy locked the front door while Lucy nodded and said something.

I couldn't help it, I wanted to see what she was up to and invite her to coffee with me if she wanted or needed emotional support this morning.

She looked up as I hurried across the street to get on her side. Thankfully the two lane road wasn't busy. A smile lit her sweet face and once again I wondered how any man could look at that beautiful face and know that sweet soul and still cheat. He had to be out of his mind.

"Hey!" I am greeted with a little wave of my mittened hand. "I didn't want to bother you, but I wanted to offer to get you a coffee if you're free."

"Oh of course! I'd love to have coffee with you." she flushed a little, glancing at the antique shop. "Please don't tell anyone?" she looked at me with those big brown eyes that reminded me of a baby dachshund. Absolutely impossible to say no to or be mad at.

"I'm not sure what you don't want me to tell them." I was clueless as to why she would be over here looking at the antique shop.

She bit her lip and looked at me, "why don't I tell you over coffee?"

I smiled. "Then let's go before someone gets our favorite spot."

She linked arms with me like we were proper ladies in the Victorian era and we headed across the street and down to the coffee shop.

Several minutes later we made ourselves comfortable in a couple of plush, tall back chairs that sat in the loft area of the café.

Lucy had asked me about the family get together and everything that I'd been trying to hold back from dumping on my friends came out. Her face displayed the same feelings I felt as I told her each part.

"I just want to spend time with them and enjoy good conversation and deepen our relationships, and maybe even receive kindness at the very least without having to prove that I'm worth it. Which of course in their minds I'm a wreck gone off the rails and need to be told how to turn my life around to reach their standards." I frowned down at my coffee and shook my head. "What I don't get is why they don't accept Gavin. I wonder if it's my fault, because he spent so much time with me and then lived with me when he was going to college instead of his parents."

Her brows furrowed, "don't ever say that. It's not your fault they don't accept him. You don't control that." she looked down and seemed to be choosing her words carefully, "it just seems that your family isn't very open minded." she peered at me under her lashes cautiously, "with all due respect. I don't mean to be too critical, they're your family."

"You're exactly right though. It just makes me feel…" I gazed off, how had we gotten to this topic?

"Empty and lonely?" She suggested.

"Exactly."

She reached over and touched my hand, "I know it's not exactly the same but please don't feel that way, you have us and we love you and we'd always be there for you. And so will Gavin. Your family might not be what they should be for you, but that doesn't mean you're alone."

I smiled, "thank you, that really helps." It was time to get this topic off of me, I had already dumped too much on her, especially for it being morning and we were only on our first cups of coffee. "Will you tell me about the antique shop?"

She got that little nervous look again and shifted in her chair. "I, uh, well I decided I needed a change. I quit my job and have sunk all my savings into opening a bookshop where the old antiques store used to be." She rushed the words out so fast I almost missed what she'd said.

I almost choked. "Wow, usually when people are going through a rough patch or changes in their life they get their hair cut or colored differently, they don't usually quit their jobs and open a store."

She flushed. "I know, but this is something I've been wanting to do for so long and it's something that this town could use. I have a business plan and everything mapped out of how I'll make money and how I'll bring customers in and how I'll handle the finances. I didn't make much at my old job so I don't need a huge amount coming in. I just want more freedom and to be happier in what I'm doing. What happened with Danny made me realize that it's not worth it to settle, career wise or otherwise."

I gazed at her, my heart swelling. "I am so proud of you for taking that step. And doing it with so much thought and planning."

She burst into tears. Oh goodness, what had I done?

Hurriedly I grabbed the napkins on the table and handed them to her, gently patting her shoulder. I didn't know what to say, clearly I could make people cry without meaning to. It was not a skill I wanted. Ro might like to have it but I was an empathetic crier and was starting to tear up myself.

"I'm sorry, I'm such a mess." Lucy dabbed at her eyes. "I've just felt so wrong after everything. And I know my parents love me and don't mean to contribute to it, but I really wish they would have picked another year to go on this cruise. I guess I would have been fine if it hadn't been for what happened with," she paused as if it was hard to say his name. "Danny."

"Don't ever be sorry for being a mess, we're all human and we all get it. And if someone acts like they don't then they're either out of touch with reality or covering themselves in a layer of armor they think will protect them. It won't. Can I just say, you used to not be able to say his name at all and now you are and you're able to confront how you feel. I think you're healing Lucy, that's really good too." I lit up at a thought, "and if you need any help with getting the space ready for the bookstore or anything, you know you can count on me."

She smiled somewhat shyly despite all the years we've known each other. "I think I'll take you up on that, if it's okay."

"I meant it. You know me. Sometimes when other people offer to help they do it because it sounds nice, not because they mean it. I am too fearful that I'll get taken up on my offer for something that I don't want to do. So as long as you promise to let me be one of the first to know about new books you're stocking, we'll call it even."

She laughed.

A shadow fell over our table and we both looked up. Be still my heart. A tall man, slim and athletic, with deep chestnut hair and dark eyes, stubble along his well defined jaw and a friendly tilt to his lips, stood over us.

"I apologize for interrupting your conversation, the barista over there, Jasmine, and I were talking and we noticed that you were crying. She said this is your favorite so I thought bringing some over might make you feel better." He gently put a box of mini strawberry cheesecake tarts on the table.

My gaze flitted from Lucy's flushed face to his handsome one. He clearly had eyes only for her though he had given me a friendly nod at the beginning of the speech.

"I can't accept that." She said timidly.

"The barista can vouch that it's safe to eat." he promised, "she watched me walk over with it."

Lucy had bright little cherries on the tops of her cheeks. "That's not what I meant at all." She paused, then gave him a shy smile. "Thank you. That was very nice of you."

"I hope it makes you feel better. And I hope to see you around town again." he nodded politely to both of us and left.

I was fairly certain there were hearts in my eyes as I watched him leave.

After we watched him walk across the room and out the door in silence we looked at each other. My excitement skyrocketed

"You have an admirer!"

Her eyes widened, "I do not, don't say that! He was just being polite"

"It's true. Did you not see the way he looked at you? I'm the one who got him just being polite with barely got a nod of hello and goodbye."

"I've never seen him before." her gaze lingered on the door.

"But he said he would see you around town. He must have moved here recently. Sounds like a mystery to ask Tammy." As the county clerk and recorder Tammy knew about everything and everyone in town. She was bubbly, outgoing, and had an eidetic memory, making her the greatest font of knowledge and gossip I'd ever met.

Lucy smiled a little then glanced at me with a mischievous glint in her eyes, "let's keep this a secret and let him remain a mystery for now."

I grinned, "my lips are sealed." I hoped she would see him again soon.

Chapter 5

The weekend rolled around and I found myself perched on a stool at a wide table, being instructed on how to make an ornament. The one held up for demonstration was glorious and made me wince. Mine would look like a homeless puppy compared to it. Gavin rubbed his hands together gleefully.

"You look like a mad scientist about to discover the zombie virus and take over humanity." Ro muttered at him. She had a point.

Madeleine had gotten wrapped up in last minute preparations for hosting her husband's parents so she hadn't ended up coming, but Lucy was perched next to us. She'd originally said that she might not be able to make it due to her new shop, but she'd gotten everything ordered and paperwork finalized so now she was just waiting to set up the shop to her liking.

Class was just about to start and a couple more people bustled in.

"Sorry we're late." Charles said as he hurried behind his daughter.

"Hi." Lucy smiled at them.

Jenny waived and they settled at another table.

Class started.

"Now let's begin with the most fundamental part of an ornament..."

Ro and I struggled, Lucy and Gavin bantered, and across from us I found myself smiling at the giggling from Jenny as her dad made outrageous choices from colors to characters he wanted on his ornament—who would have thought of putting Mr. Magoo from Mr. Magoo's Christmas Carol, on an ornament?

Nearly an hour later I determined that Ro and I had no talent, and Lucy and Gavin would need to carry on the torch of the arts for us.

"What is that?" Ro pointed at a spot of paint on my ornament.

I peered at it. "A finch."

Her eyebrows shot up and she peered closer. "Cammie, that is not a finch. It looks like a centipede."

"Yours isn't exactly Van Gogh." I grumbled.

"Did someone call me Van Gogh?" Gavin perked up, holding his tiny paintbrush in the air with a flourish.

"Yours does look lovely." Lucy said.

Ro and I exchanged glances.

"Is it fair to hate them?" I whispered.

"Yes."

The teacher moved around, giving advice and encouragement to the students. When she got around to our table she cooed over Gavin's creation.

"So much talent! What a wonderful idea. Oh an Lucy, your angel is so detailed. It's hard to create such a beautiful picture on your first try on the ball shape of an ornament, congratulations!" she stepped over to Ro and I.

I gulped.

"Oh my. It looks like you two had fun." She left.

Ro glowered after her. "She could at least have *pretended*." She grumbled.

"Clearly she favors young people."

"Cammie, we didn't have creative talent when we were young either."

"Fine, fine. Kill any bit of pride I could possibly have left."

Gavin turned to look at us. "How are you two doing?" He peered at my ornament. "What is that?" He pointed.

"A centipede." Ro supplied helpfully.

"Huh." He shrugged, "it's original, I like it."

"See." I elbowed Ro.

She pursed her lips and gave me a look that said I was childish and unrealistic. Little did she know I had already accepted that about myself and it could no longer be used against me.

At the end of the class we packed up our completed ornaments in white gift boxes and agreed to meet at the parade this evening.

"Come on." I wiggled past other people in thick coats and mittens, carrying steaming to-go cups of cocoa as they waited for the festivities to unfold. Meanwhile, shop signs flashed and windows had been decorated to draw people in, promising discounts and the most delicious treats you'd ever taste. Some people had even set up booths inside some of the shops, selling their own homemade trinkets with a percent going to the shop for the space. I had been dragged into several of those traps by Gavin and now the entire back seat of my car was filled with packages.

Being a tourist town not a lot of people lived here, but people loved to come to our events so the street was packed out with attendees eager to shop and watch the spectacular parade.

"Look at this mass of humanity. Its glorious." Gavin was keeping up behind me even as I dodged around clusters of people. Ro had claimed a spot in front of the crowd, closest to the street so we could see the floats better.

"You can say that because you're tall and can see where we're going. I'm just picking a direction and hoping it's right."

"Oh, I didn't realize that. Then I should tell you we've been traveling away from the ladies."

I stopped so suddenly he flailed so he didn't run into me. When I turned to him his mischievous grin let me know that he was teasing me.

"You're getting coal." I told him and started to push through the throng of people again.

He laughed.

We finally made it to Ro whose unfriendly gaze was keeping enough space around her for us to squeeze into. Lucy was already there and she turned and embraced Gavin.

"I'm so glad you stayed for this!"

"I'm glad you came. Look at that red nose, are you trying out to be Rudolph?" He had two scarves twisted in elegant ways around his face and neck and he took one off, draping it over her neck and then wrapping it over her face like a face mask.

"But you'll be cold." She protested, voice muffled by the fabric.

"Oh believe me, he has enough layers on that he'll be fine. He only wore that second scarf for looks." I assured her. I'd watched him fuss over what to wear for thirty minutes before reminding him that no one would see his outfit under his big coat. He'd bemoaned that the only way he'd get to be stylish was to add accessories to his outfit. Thus the two scarves, matching red beanie and mittens, and small circular gold earrings.

Just then Madeliene shoved through the crowd, making it to us with a huff. "Who invited all these people? A lady can't even get breathing room." She grumbled.

"You look lovely as always." Gavin said. He peered at her hair, a few curls that escaped her cap. "Darling, are you going grey?"

If Madeleine's cheeks weren't already red they would be with that question.

"I'm thinking about it. Your cousin keeps telling me natural is easiest and still beautiful."

"Hmm. I could give you a frost and strip some of the darker color to help you grow it out without an obvious line of color."

"That might work, I'll think about it." She turned toward the street. "This parade needs to start soon, it's freezing."

"Where are your husband and his parents?" Ro asked.

Madeleine arched a delicate eyebrow at her. "Trying to get rid of me so soon?" She didn't let her answer. "Lawrence took his parents home because it was too cold for them despite the knee-length parkas, mittens, hats, scarves, and even face masks we'd stuffed them in."

Music started and the whole crowd seemed to hold its collective breath while we waited for the first float to appear. A police car started the procession with lights flashing.

Here the floats came. There was a Deocrated Forest float which consisted of several decorated fir trees, a Gingerbread House float, a float that was decorated like a house and had someone in a grinch costume doing a darn good job of sneaking around the float and stuffing the presents and decorations into a bag, then came a Candy Land float with people tossing out handfuls of candy. Several more paraded past. Finally, bringing up the rear, was Santa and Mrs. Clause on a sleigh being pulled by a couple of horses with fake antlers attached to their heads.

"That's Charles Sturm, Jenny's dad." Lucy told us. "They were the dad and daughter at the ornament class." She told Gavin. "He's a single dad and is a banker so he's always busy, but he finds ways to give back to the community. Such a nice guy."

"Seems like a good dad, too." I watched him stand and wave to kids on both sides of the street, laughing a jolly laugh that had to come from his belly. It made me smile.

The sleigh passed, ending the parade.

"Ugh, I drank too much cocoa before this." Gavin turned but couldn't possibly see much past the throng of people, despite his height. "I wonder where the closest powder room is."

"Probably in that shop." Lucy gestured vaguely. "I can lead the way."

"We'll be right back." Gavin promised before striding after her.

"We might be at the coffee shop." Madeleine called after them. She turned back Ro and I. "It's ridiculously cold."

I hummed my agreement. My breath came out in puffs that floated in front of my face and despite my winter gear I shivered. "I vote we go to the coffee shop to wait for them."

"Sounds good to me." Ro led the way with Madeliene and I trailing. Further down the sidewalk I stopped to fiddle with the laces on my tall winter boots. I needed shorter laces for the darned things, and I'd had that same thought every winter for the last three years. Clearly I was a woman of action.

I straightened and hurried to catch up with the ladies who were several yards ahead of me.

"Oof." I huffed as someone smashed into my side. They pushed away from me and I turned around indignantly. They could at least be polite.

It was an elf who had jumped out of the Santa's Shop doorway, shoving past me before stumbling. Even as I opened my mouth to scold him, he clutched his chest.

The elf collapsed into a rumpled heap on the ground.

"Are you okay?" What kind of a stupid question was that?

Another elf darted out of the shop, froze for a split second at the sight, then hurried away through the crowd.

I collected my frazzled thoughts. "Sir, please respond if you're conscious, I'm calling an ambulance for you."

When I didn't get a response I hurried over.

"Cammie?" I heard Ro and Madeleine coming back to me. Other people started to come over as I knelt by the man.

Oh. It was the same guy from the holiday fair.

"Sir?" I shook him.

Ro knelt down on the other side of the unconscious form and put two fingers on his neck.

"Does he need CPR?" someone asked.

I glanced up at the speaker. Behind him Santa had come to see what was going on, and now he turned away, back into the crowd.

"No, but he does need us to call 9-1-1." Ro said, serious gaze meeting mine. I froze, realizing what she meant.

"I'm dialing them now." Madeleine said.

I looked back at the dead man. Frowning, I focused on his clothes where a dark spot spread on his outfit. I pulled at the clothing. It came away from his body, sticky, and revealed a slim, deep hole in his chest. I recoiled.

Madeleine bent down near me. "Yes, he's unconscious."

Dead. Ro mouthed.

Madeliene's eyes widened. "He doesn't have a pulse." When she hung up she huddled close. "What on earth happened?"

Ro gazed at him solemnly. "It looks like he's been murdered."

We had waited for the police by the body, shielding him from nosy people. Now that whole part of the street was blocked off and we were told to stay in the area so they could talk to us. Joy. We went into the coffee shop so we could sit down and get a reprieve from the cold. Though right now all I felt was numb.

"I can't believe I've been Cammie'd." Madeleine quipped sourly.

"Hey," I snapped out of my daze and sat up, indignant, "You may not use me as a verb. It's not my fault I've found two people who'd been murdered."

"Okay." Ro stood. "I'm going to go order us all something." she looked at Madeleine. "What would you like, a cookie, chamomile tea, a tranquilizer?"

Madeleine slumped in her chair with a dramatic groan.

"Chamomile tea it is. I'll see if they have some Valium to add to it. Cammie?"

How could I think of anything besides what we'd just seen. "Just water, please."

Ro left the table.

More and more people gathered outside, revealed by the big front windows, and inside, curious about the police presence. Gossip was loudly whispered from person to person.

Lucy and Gavin made their way through the crowd to us.

"We were gone for only fifteen minutes, what happened?" Lucy asked, eyes wide. Madeleine waved at her to sit.

I brought them up to speed as Gavin stole a chair from another table and sat down next to me.

"Oh my goodness." Lucy breathed when I was done.

"Hold onto your hats everyone, we have a Christmas crisis on our hands."

"Gavin!" I hissed.

"It's hardly your fault a nasty person was found dead."

I blinked. "How did you know he was a nasty person?"

"There was a grumpy old man talking to a young woman. She asked him why he wasn't staying for the parade and he said he hated Christmas. Then he saw the guy, who I'm assuming is the same person, come running past in an elf costume and he said he hated that, and I quote, *jackaninny*, so much because he was a con artist."

A con artist. I filed that information away for later. Not that there would be a "later."

A new police officer, tall and trim in his uniform with an elegant, dark sable Belgian Malinois next to him, strode into the café. He cast his dark gaze around the room and it landed on us like a hammer.

"Oh." Lucy's eyes rounded.

"Now we know who he is." I muttered.

The same man who had given Lucy that pastry the other day marched toward us like the grim reaper with his hell hound.

Chapter 6

The officer stopped at our table, casting his gaze around at each of us, lingering on Lucy.

He cleared his throat. "I'm Lucas Baker, I'm here to investigate what happened out there. I was told one of you found the body?"

Madeleine pointed at me, "that would be Cammie," causing him to pin me with his beautiful and a bit frightening gaze.

I waved my hands in front of me defensively. "Ro and Madeleine were with me when I found him. We all found him at the same time really. In fact, Ro was the one who had the foresight to check his pulse."

She didn't look uncomfortable at all when his gaze swung around to her. In fact she looked more relaxed than I'd seen her in a while. Ah yes, after how many years in the CIA she would be familiar with dealing with questioning. I assumed, not that I would ever know for sure since she never talked about her past life.

"I'd like to take each of you and speak with you separately." he glanced around. All the tables were taken.

He quickly walked a few tables over to a small one in the corner, said something to the people sitting there and came back as they scurried away. "Cammie, I would like to speak to you first."

Madeleine owed me a Christmas cheesecake for that sellout. I dutifully trailed him to the table and settled in the seat. I had no reason to be nervous, none at all, but after being yelled at by the chief so many times during the investigation of the bones at the manor a few months back I braced for more annoyance directed my way.

"Can I call you Cammie or would you like to be called Ms.?" He raised his eyebrows at me.

"My last name is Lockett but please call me Cammie."

"Okay Cammie, can you walk me through what happened? Please include every detail that you remember regarding the victim and surroundings."

Should I tell him what I'd heard about that man? No, I would stick to what I'd seen today.

I told him about how the elf ran out of the Santa's Shop store, and how another elf had run out of the building after him and then disappeared in the crowd after seeing him collapse.

"Can you give me any distinctions? Height, build?" his pen was poised, ready.

I thought back. "It was a very petite person. It must have been a woman. Of course I didn't see her face or anything but she was shorter than me with a very slight build." I frowned, thinking about it. "It could have been a short, skinny guy as well."

He nodded along, taking notes, not making me feel like I was a fool and a hindrance. That was nice. I hoped that I got to deal with him and not the chief in the future.

"Okay, go on."

"I didn't see anything else, I was too focused on him. I thought maybe he had low blood sugar and needed food or something. Ro came over and touched his neck, checking for a pulse. She told me there was none and then I saw a dark stain on his clothes. Or what I had thought was a dark stain until I pulled his shirt away and showed that it was a terrible injury to his chest."

"Did you see anyone around that looked suspicious or out of place besides the elf who was running in the opposite direction?"

I thought about it carefully, trying to rerun through every moment leading up to that. Had anyone in the surrounding crowd acted strange? I frowned. Santa—Charles Strum—had come up and then moved away. Maybe he just didn't like the sight of blood.

"It seems you might have thought of something?" he was watching me carefully. *Now* he made me nervous. The chief was never that discerning. Or maybe I was just overly emoting right now.

"I saw someone leaving after Ro checked Darwin's pulse. It could be it was just very upsetting for him." I hurried to say.

"Darwin," he scribbled the name down. "Do you have a last name?"

"No, I only know his first."

"Do you know who the person leaving the area was?"

I sighed, he'd catch me if I lied, and I didn't want to. "Santa. But I know he had nothing to do with it."

"Did you have eyes on him before you saw the victim?"

I had thought through what I remembered a few times now. "No."

He wrote that down.

"But that doesn't mean anything." I added.

He looked up and gave me a close lipped smile that still managed to be comforting. "I'm not accusing anyone of anything. I'm just gathering puzzle pieces to get a good picture of what happened."

That was good. "Thank you."

"It's my job Ms. Cammie."

I didn't mention that it was the chief's job too and he didn't...oh never mind. It did no good to dwell on things one couldn't change. And I only had a few dealings with him, and those had been when he was particularly stressed with a murder, so I had to give him some grace for that.

"Do you know the person who was in the Santa suit?"

I swallowed audibly. There went any chance of saying I didn't know and being convincing. I didn't want poor Charles to be suspected of anything.

"His name is Charles Sturm. But I know he didn't do anything, he has a young daughter to take care of."

He asked me a couple more questions and then asked me to send Ro over.

I sat down as Ro left the table.

"What was he like?" Lucy asked.

Madeleine said at the same time, "how was he?"

"First off, he has beautiful eyes. Second, he's smart and discerning. He has a good, stable job and is very courteous. Also, he's tall."

"Goodness Cammie, it sounds like you're setting up a dating profile for him." Madeleine said.

I gestured at Lucy, "he's handsome, unattached, and new in town. He needs friends to help him settle in."

"Friends, huh?" Madeleine gave me a skeptical look. "And how do you know he's unattached?"

"Things he's said."

"Way to be mysterious."

Lucy watched us bicker with a peculiar look on her face.

"How did that man die?"

I blinked, the harsh reality I didn't want to dwell on came to the forefront. "He had some type of stab wound on his chest that I saw when I pulled his shirt away from his body."

"Oh that's awful. I wonder why anyone would want to kill him?" Lucy looked sad.

"I have a feeling that he wasn't well liked."

"What makes you say that?" Madeleine leaned forward.

"I've seen him before. He doesn't seem like a nice man. Kind of smarmy. Plus I heard from a couple of people that he wasn't an upstanding person." It briefly crossed my mind that perhaps I should have told officer Baker about the incident with Anthony Blake. No, that could just stir up unnecessary drama. I hadn't even seen the attorney at the parade today.

"If he were someone that was unlikable that does open up a larger pool of people who could have killed them." Madeleine mused.

I nodded, "it was such a big crowd too. And honestly why would he be in that elf costume? I heard him speak very derisively about the parade and Christmas in general being for chumps."

"Chumps!" Madeleine straightened up in her chair in indignation.

"So isn't it odd that he was it an elf costume?"

Madeleine drummed her fingers on the table. "I wonder who might have seen him right before he died."

"Can I just say something?" Lucy said with a raised hand. "The police are on it, so we should just leave it to them."

It shouldn't have made me feel unneeded, but it did. Surely it would be of some help for us to find any information we could regarding this case.

"You're right Lucy, of course. I think the last dead body Cammie came across got us into a destructive mindset when it comes to these things."

"Why do you sound like you're accusing me? I'm completely innocent here."

Madeleine gave me a flat look, "face it Cammie, you have a penchant for trouble."

Before I could think of a withering reply, Ro reappeared.

"Your turn." she nodded at Madeleine.

Just then, Gavin came back with a drink carrier and a box full of little pastries. "That line was murder." He set everything on the table and sat down.

"Too soon." Madeleine said even as the rest of us chuckled at the pun.

Madeleine headed off to talk with officer Baker.

"Poor luck." Gavin said, peering at Lucy over his mug. "If you hadn't been so chivalrous in helping me find a powder room you could have been there for the murder."

Lucy's eyes widened "why would that be a good thing?"

"You could be talking to Mr. Hunky over there."

"Gavin!" Lucy blushed.

Ro smirked and I stared into my mug, the cocoa obscured by tiny white puffs of marshmallows rising in a mountain on top of it. Around it was a pretty ring of whipped cream. If the marshmallows were red and the top one was white it would look like a Santa's hat. I would have to suggest that to Jasmine.

"Lucy, tell me about that store you're opening. You got interrupted by that inconvenient murder."

All I could do was shake my head. Gavin was as irreverent as Ro. But his was in an effort to cheer us up while hers was just her cut and dry approach to everything.

Ro perked up as his words and looked at Lucy. Lucy picked at a cranberry scone, a little smile on her lips as she thought about something. We all waited.

"Cammie knows about this, but I quit my job and have rented the place the antique shop used to be in. I did all the ordering and everything and I'm opening up a bookstore." She glanced at Ro under her lashes as if she expected judgment.

"You're going to need help renovating the inside for a bookshop." Was all she said.

Ro was many things, practical, overly direct, sometimes socially unaware—or perhaps it was that she just didn't care—but she always supported us after fussing about how illogical our actions were. It was more than my family, my mom, would do. They would fuss and continue to fuss. How long had it been since I'd moved from the city? Over a decade? They still judged my decision.

I shook off the melancholy and grinned. "I cannot wait to see Madeleine's face when she hears that we're renovating another space." I glanced at Lucy, "that is if you want the help, or the hindrance, however you look at it. At least we'll be there to support you if you want."

She laughed. "I love you guys."

Ro grumbled something about mushy people under her breath as Gavin and I simultaneously said, "we love you too!"

Madeleine and officer Baker made their way over.

"It's been determined that none of you are the killer so that's good news." Lucas Baker said. He didn't smile but his eyes crinkled with good humor and he glanced at Lucy before quickly looking away.

"You can never be too sure, Lucy looks rather suspicious to me." Ro said.

Lucy's cheeks turned a cheery cherry color and she looked like she wanted to slide under the table. If officer Baker hadn't been there I might have just started chuckling. As it was I managed to keep myself from embarrassing Lucy further.

He smiled. Oh my he had a beautiful smile. "I'll make sure to keep an eye on you." He had the audacity to wink at her.

Despite her clear embarrassment Lucy held his gaze and gave him a sweet smile. "I'll expect to see you around then."

His smile deepened and he nodded goodbye at us before heading out.

"Wow, Lucy. If you don't take him I think Cammie will. She practically swooned when he winked." Gavin chuckled wickedly.

"Just for that you're going to the rest of the family holiday events without me." I grumbled.

"There there." he patted my hand. "No need for vengeance."

"What a day." Madeleine snagged a pastry from the box Gavin had brought over. "I don't think there's ever been such an eventful parade. And our Christmas parade is always extremely popular."

I had to agree with her. "And we got amazing news from Lucy too."

Madeleine blinked. "Did I miss officer handsome asking you out?"

"No but you did miss the part where we promised we would all pitch in and help renovate another space." Ro said. She and Gavin were on a roll today. It wasn't Halloween, no one needed to play the Wicked Witch of the West.

Madeleine's expression went stone cold as she pinned an amused Ro with her stare. "Explain." Her tone made me want to jump up and rush to the nearest bomb shelter. After the whole thing with renovating the manor for an event that could help us raise money for the historical society and finding the dead body and then solving the crime and then ending up not having needed to put all that work into the ballroom in the first place Madeleine was fairly put out with any form of physical labor.

Lucy's eyes grew round and she glanced at me. I made a scooping motion in her direction with my hands. She was the one who could calm this fire before it started.

"I quit my job." She blurted.

Madeleine's gaze went from Ro to Lucy who squirmed under it. "And you started a construction business that you expect us to help with?"

Gavin and I chuckled, earning us a scowl.

"No, no, of course not. Ro was just being dramatic. I have rented the space that the antique shop used to be in and I'm opening a bookstore. Ro and Cammie just said they would help me set things up if needed. It's not necessary though. And it shouldn't be that much work, just some décor and the furniture, the inside is already pretty nice."

Understanding dawned on Madeleine's face and she reached out and put her hand on top of Lucy's. "Honey, are you sure you're going to be okay financially?"

Realistically, that should have probably been my first question. But I'd had my ideas and dreams trampled on so many times when expressing them that I couldn't bear to bring reality in to dissolve her happiness. If she needed help we would all help her.

Lucy gave her a big smile. "I have a little nest egg. This is truly what I want to do and I did my research and a business plan and all of that so I really think it will do well. It'll be a little bit of a gift shop too, so it won't just be books and it'll attract more tourists in."

"That was smart." Ro said. And this time it wasn't her usual dry sarcasm, she meant it.

We chatted more, calming our adrenaline raised from the death that had happened in front of us, and then we all bid each other goodnight. Gavin was incredibly busy as he was popular enough to have at least fifteen Christmas parties he was invited to outside of the family's, so he didn't stay the night.

He'd left his car in my driveway and we'd taken my vehicle so I drove him back and helped him load his avalanche of packages into his trunk. Outside his car he leaned down and gave me a peck on the cheek. "I missed this. You and I used to do things like this more often when I was in college and lived with you."

"See people get murdered?" I joked.

He laughed. "That's a new one."

I reached up and gave my tall, skinny cousin a big hug. "You know you're welcome anytime. All you have to do is text me or call me and let me know that you're coming. And if you come without saying anything I wouldn't mind either. As long as you don't have any other family members with you." I winked.

He laughed. "I may take you up on that before this holiday is over."

I waited until he left, waving as he drove away.

Inside the house Rutherford marched up to me and got upon his hind legs as he stretched his front paws up on my leg.

"Are you protesting? You've been getting fat buddy, I don't think that you're going to starve anytime soon."

I walked into the kitchen and got him his dinner. I pulled a salad from the fridge. I wasn't giving up and resorting to eating rabbit food, it was a Christmas salad with various fruits, seeds, and a sweet vinaigrette. I could barely tell that there was salad in there.

My home phone rang right next to me, causing me to nearly drop the bowl.

"Hello?"

"Cammie, I'm so glad I caught you. I'm sorry to be calling late with a request." Susie, the reason the animal shelter operated as well as it did, had a sweet voice and she always sounded apologetic. Even when she didn't need to.

"It's not that late." I assured her, smiling so she could hear the warmth over the phone. "What can I help you with?"

"I need a foster over Christmas for a cat we just got in."

I squeezed my eyes shut and then glanced over at Rutherford. He'd finished eating and was now sitting, staring at me as he licked his paw. When I looked over at him he paused his licking and eyed me as if I were up to something evil. In his mind this would be.

"Of course I could take a cat. Is it a kitten?"

"No, it's a full grown, house trained cat. In good shape, but her owner just passed away and there's no family to take her."

It was a her, that was good. Despite being neutered of course, Rutherford could still be territorial. He was even fussy with me when I reached for one of his favorite shoe boxes in my closet. He never scratched me but he did smack my hand a few times.

"When do you need me to pick her up?"

"If you can take her now, I'll bring her over." She said eagerly.

"I'll be ready and waiting."

"Thank you so much!"

I got a baggie of treats—the human kind—ready for Susie.

When she came in we did an exchange. She got the treats and I got the beautiful, cuddly cat. As soon as she came into my arms she put her paws around my neck in what could have been a hug. If it had been Rutherford I would know for sure that it was a stranglehold, not a hug. But this cat started purring as she laid her head against my neck. What a precious little thing.

"What's her name?"

Susie set down a few items, a bag of cat treats, a half full bag of cat food, a couple of toys.

"I don't know. The police in the city got called because of the person who'd passed away and they discovered that no one was there to take the cat so she went to animal control and of course they're absolutely packed as usual so they called me. Feel free to give her whatever name you'd like."

"Hmm. Okay, thank you Susie." I made sure she had her bag of baked items and waved goodbye.

I looked down in time to meet Rutherford's accusatory glare.

"You can be gracious for one Christmas."

I carried the cat into my room and set her on my bed. Rutherford followed close on my heels, jumped up on the other side of the bed, and stared at the villainous intruder.

"Be nice." I said sternly.

I went into my closet to grab a pair of pajamas. The music box caught my attention. I could have sworn that I'd covered it back up with the cloth. Reaching up I pulled it down and gently traced one of the patterns carved into the wood so beautifully with my finger. A mystery to solve, I would have to do some research when I went back to work. I wrapped the box up and put it back.

Turning around I flinched and let out a scream.

Chapter 7

Both cats had already vanished from the room and I stood face to face was someone I didn't recognize. I did recognize that it was a ghost. My heart, slamming against my rib cage as aggressively as possible, recognized it as a threat. Wait, just wait. The ghosts from the manor hand never touched us or moved anything solid. So it was likely that this ghost couldn't either. Or wouldn't.

We stared at each other. It was a man, dressed in an old suit, a chain went from the middle of his vest to a small pocket. A pocket watch? The suit had to be made of wool, it looked of good quality with a thick overcoat and trousers, a vest underneath and a button up shirt underneath that. His shoes were dark, possibly leather. I stopped my perusal to look at his face, hopefully I hadn't offended him. Could ghosts get offended? It looked like he was standing on the floor but I knew for a fact that he could float, if the other ghosts that I'd encountered were any indication. His hair was long, longer than I would assume would be respectable for a businessman in the era I imagined he came from. He had a bit of face stubble and a goatee. His eyes were kind as he looked at me.

"Um, what do you need?" I was still convinced that the ghosts had helped us solve Alan Garrett's murder only a few months ago, so they must have had some cognition, even if I've never heard them speak.

His gaze left my face and he focused in on the wrapped music box on the shelf behind me. Then he looked back at me, held my gaze for an instant, and vanished.

Well that wasn't alarming. I took deep breaths to try and calm myself and then went in search of the cats.

Holly, as I had decided to call her, was hiding behind my love seat while Rutherford had taken up residence in the corner of the kitchen counter, next to the cookie jar. His gaze was now both accusatory and resentful.

"That wasn't my fault." I told him.

But maybe it was. Why had he looked at the box? Maybe he was somehow attached to the box, tasked with looking after it. Or maybe it had belonged to him. Whatever it was, I needed to do some research on that box. I was planning to do that anyway but now it was urgent. I couldn't have random ghosts popping into my life. I was still trying to come to terms with everything from a few months ago. It felt surreal now and if the ladies hadn't also born witness to the ghosts, I might have convinced myself I had dreamed it all.

I would be at work tomorrow, so I could do my research then. The day after that I would be off so I could help with the drive for donations of toys for children that were in need.

It was so quiet during Christmastime at the Cultural Arts Center slash archive slash historical society that it would be easy for me to do my research.

I stood by the phone for a minute, wondering if I should call one of the ladies. Or all of them. No, I needed to do some investigating first. Even though having a ghost appear in my bedroom was alarming, so far they'd all been nonviolent. As if I was an expert after encountering two at the manor.

I coaxed the cats back into my room with cat treats. They weren't nearly as good as dogs in the capacity of being an alarm should anyone or anything up here in my room again, but the way they booked it out of there made me think that at least I would be alerted to another intrusion.

I settled back against my pillows. In an act of defiance Rutherford hopped over and jumped on my stomach, curling his tail around his feet as he sat there.

"No." I scooped him off. "I can see right through you. Be nice to Holly."

Finally everyone settled down. Holly came up and curled against me, kneading my arm. Rutherford sat rather than lay and stared at us. I reached my hand toward him but he would have none of it and ended up curling up on the other side of the bed.

Morning came with no more frightening incidents and after getting ready I scooped up the music box and carried it to my car.

I had decorated the Cultural Arts Center for Christmas. I had updated the different displays with items that various cultures and eras used for the Christmas season, on the door was a traditional wreath with a yellow satin bow wrapped around it, complementing the fake poinsettias. On my desk was a tiny glass tree with equally delicate glass ornaments.

I only had a few pressing matters to get to before I could start my research. With those aside, and after dealing with a phone call—someone trying to reach the courthouse—I grabbed the box, still wrapped, and headed to the archives. The bell over the door would let me know if someone came in.

The archive room was windowless and housed aged documents that detailed all the goings-on of this part of the state for the last seventy years. I had set a table on one side of the room so anyone doing research could comfortably spread their documents out. Now I placed the box on it gingerly. That done, I decided on the criteria I would use to search. Thirty years ago or more, woodworking businesses. I made my way over to the shelves that held details of the businesses that had come and gone through the years.

Time to get to work.

Three immersive hours later and I needed to rest my eyes. I had the names of several people and shops that had popped up throughout the many years, and now it was time to go track down some people who could help answer my questions about what kind of woodworking they did back then. I also planned to do an internet search to see if I could find a similar box anywhere else so I could learn more about it and who could possibly have the skill to do this work.

With my stack of papers in hand I picked up the box and looked back at the archives to make sure I'd placed everything else back in order. I jumped at the sight of the ghost hovering near the shelving unit that I had just left.

"What the heck." I muttered, clutching the box closer to me. I watched him and he returned my gaze solemnly. When he didn't move I finally broke eye contact and left the room. What else was I to do? I shut the door to the archive—he wouldn't be getting stuck in there—and headed up toward my office. I couldn't help but glance over my shoulder. He was following me. I pivoted around and stared at him, he stopped.

"Is there something I can do for you?" Maybe a stupid question to ask a ghost, but why was he following me? It was unnerving, to say the least. If he was going to keep showing up I needed to tell the ladies. Well, I didn't need to, but for my own peace of mind I wanted to. Despite all we'd been through and seen this last winter I still wanted confirmation that I wasn't going mad.

Again he didn't move anywhere, just stood there waiting for... I'm not sure what. I unwrapped the box and showed it to him. "Do you know who carved this and who owned it?"

His gaze dropped to the box and he floated forward a foot, then stopped, still several feet away from me and stared at the box. That was helpful.

It was strange, but not frightening. When he didn't make another move I turned around and walked up the stairs to my little office. On the landing before I stepped through the door I glanced back to see if he'd followed again. He was gone. So strange.

Several minutes and a lot of reading later and my phone rang. I reached across the desk and snagged it off of its receiver.

"Cultural Arts Center, this is Cammie." I answered absent mindedly, still reading an article that talked about a competition that was held among various craftsmen in the area decades ago.

"Hi, it's me." Lucy said.

I stopped reading. "Hey Lucy, is everything okay?"

"Of course it is, I didn't mean to worry you. I just, um, I got the shipment of shelves and décor in and I was wondering if you would have any time to help set up? Of course if you're busy that's totally fair, I completely understand."

"Of course I'll help you. When do you want me there?"

"Could you help me start tonight?" She sounded hesitant.

"Sure thing. Right after work? I can bring pizza or sandwiches."

"That's so nice, but you shouldn't have to get food for all of us, Madeleine and Ro will be there too. Well at least Madeleine will be, I still haven't gotten ahold of Ro."

"Ro has no family and no friends besides us, she'll be there." I said, amused. "I'll get us pizza."

"Thank you!" she sounded so excited that it made me smile. "I'll pay you back."

"No need. I can't wait to see what you have planned for your new store."

"You're the best."

We hung up and I went back to my research.

A few hours later I was at Mizza's Pizzas Staring at a terrifying concoction that was supposed to be a Christmas pizza. Should pizza have gingerbread on it? And what was that green sauce? I peered closer. Was that pesto?

"Are you sure you don't want to try it?" Tina asked.

"As tempting as it looks," I only just managed to keep from shuddering, "I think I'll just stick with a small cheese and a small supreme."

"They'll be out in about fifteen minutes."

"Thank you."

I pulled the phone I hated from my purse to do some internet searches. Gavin and Ro were always telling me I needed to stop hiding from technology, that I wasn't old enough to have the excuse not to know. But I'd always been an old soul and purposely lived in a small town to save myself the hassle of fast city life. Which definitely included being connected to the internet twenty-four seven.

I had a text message.

Gavin: *They want to have a Twelve Days of Christmas themed party next.*

I typed back: *I think I'll be sick that weekend.*

Actually, it sounded fun and I wanted to see everyone dressed up and happy.

Gavin sent back a laughing face and I went back to my research.

It turned out that the music box was likely worth between one thousand and several thousand. Helpful. Even though the music box wasn't worth that back then a master craftsman would have been known and it would be recorded somewhere. I hoped, given how long ago it was. If only that ghost could have just said this is where the box came from and this is who it belonged to. Then I could reach out to the person who inherited it. The original owner was likely gone by now.

My musing was interrupted when Charles and his daughter Jenny walked in and ordered a pizza and a tub of cookie dough. Tina took their order and they proceeded to wait in the little front area with me.

"How are you?" I asked. I contained a wince as I remembered that he had seen what happened at the parade. I certainly hope she hadn't.

Charles glanced at me cautiously then a little smile touched his lips, "Cammie right, Lucy's friend?"

I smiled. "Yes, that's me.

"That's right, you were at the parade." He sobered.

Jenny's eyes went wide as she looked at me, "weren't you the one who found Darwin?"

"Jenny, that's not appropriate." Her father scolded.

"That's alright." I quickly intervened. "I'm sorry for what happened to that man, and I'm also sorry that the evening of celebrating and shopping got cut short because of it. What did you think of that whole incident?" he'd been there, I'd seen him. And like I told the officer, he had seen the body and then hurried away.

"A horrible thing to happen." He said.

"Dad and I were together when it happened. He kept me from seeing though." Jenny said quickly.

"That was good of your dad, it was a sad thing to see."

"He wasn't a very nice man though. So it wasn't that sad." The girl said matter of factly.

Charly put his hand over his face before he looked at me with apologetic eyes, "she didn't mean that."

"From what I've heard it's not untrue." I said, hoping to console him. Sometimes kids just spoke the truth, unhindered by social expectations, as strange as they may be.

The pizzas came out, along with a complimentary breadsticks, and I thanked Tina, said goodbye to the other two, and left.

This time of night it was easy to find a parking spot on Main Street next to the antique store. I couldn't believe Mildred and Earl had finally decided to close up and move to some place with a beach. Or that Lucy had decided to undertake a new venture. Out of all of us, for her to take such a step and not stay in the confines of safety of her nine to five was incredible. Inside there were boxes and boxes of items, big ones probably indicating shelving units that needed to be put together. The building itself was well taken care of, the inside already renovated beautifully, with glistening dark floors and clean white walls. It looked like new windows were also installed recently.

"Are you opening before Christmas?" Madeleine was asking when I pushed through the door.

"I want to. It really depends how far we get with it. Thank you again for your help."

They turned when I walked in, likely smelling the savory pizzas.

"You made it." Lucy smiled.

"Of course." I set the items down. "Looks like there's a lot to get done in here."

"It's a bit overwhelming."

The door *tinged* and Ro walked in. Her scarf covered the bottom half of her face but her nose was reminiscent of a cherry. She must have walked here.

"You look like you just came from the North Pole." Madeleine quipped.

"It's even colder out there now that the sun has gone down." She unwound her scarf and put her jacket with the rest of ours on a coat rack Lucy had set near the door. "Did any of you see the Newspaper? That murder is all over. Even in the library I kept hearing people talking about what a horrid man that Darwin was."

"Just because someone wasn't likeable doesn't necessarily mean there are a lot of people who would kill him. It's such a violent act." I said, starting to cut open one of the boxes with the box cutter and Lucy had left on a table.

"Wouldn't it have to be a really personal motivation for someone to kill him?" Lucy asked, helping me get the box open.

"Like him being a con man?" I mused.

Ro gave me a look, "I suppose next to jealousy, money is probably the biggest motivator in murder."

"That's why my husband doesn't have me on his life insurance policy." Madeleine said, deadpan. When I looked over her eyes were crinkled with amusement.

The rest of us laughed.

A gentle tap sounded at the door and I jumped higher than I probably needed to, my mind going back to the uninvited visitor I'd had in my room last night and then in the Cultural Arts Center while I was working. We all turn toward the door.

"Come in?" Lucy said, uncertainly, glancing at Ro. I was with her on that. If something bad happened we all trusted Ro would tackle the intruder.

The door was pushed open and a familiar face appeared. Lucas Baker looked sheepish as he stepped in and looked around the shop. His well behaved dog stepped in and sat next to him, looking at us with interest. Weather it was interest because he thought we were food or interest because he thought we were drug dealers that he could bite, or interest because he liked to be petted, I would not be going over to find out.

"I didn't mean to intrude, I just wanted to make sure everything was alright since I saw a light on and as far as I knew there wasn't anyone renting this space."

"That's okay, I'm renting it now, thank you for checking." Lucy said sweetly.

Ro cocked an eyebrow, "you're doing checks on places in your civilian clothes?"

He chuckled. "You caught me, I'm not on shift but wanted to check it out anyway."

"Well since you're here, Lucy should tell you about her plans for this shop. You haven't been here long, maybe she can tell you more about the town too." Madeleine said, looking rather sly.

Lucy flushed while he smiled.

"It looks like you're busy. Tell you what, if you have time, do you want to meet up for coffee and bring me up to speed on the town happenings?"

Lucy hesitated a moment.

"Of course, it looks like you're busy so I wouldn't fault you at all for needing to focus on this." He said, giving her an easy out. Nice guy. I was liking him more and more, even though he was a part of the police department.

"No, I would like that. To have coffee I mean." Her cheeks reddened. "To talk about the town of course. It's the least I can do for a new officer."

He had a dimple when he smiled. "Will you give me your number so we can coordinate?"

She gave him her number and then he said goodbye to all of us and left.

"Oh I do really like him." Madeleine said, humming in her throat approvingly.

"Madeleine!" Lucy said as though she were scandalized. She wore a happy expression I hadn't seen since the scoundrel who should not be named had broken her heart just over six months ago.

"That was a surprising twist to the night." Ro said with a little smirk Lucy's way.

"There's no way that's more surprising than a ghost showing up in your bedroom." I muttered, my mind taken me back to the interruption I'd had. I turned back to the work I'd been in the middle of. I finished fixing the shelf onto the wall and turned to grab another piece, only to find everyone staring at me, aghast.

"What did you just say Cammie?" Madeleine demanded.

Oh had I ever just opened a can of worms with that comment.

"The Ghost of Christmas Past decided to visit me. He scared the bejeebers out of my cats."

They kept staring at me. Why did this always happen to me?

Ro cocked an eyebrow. "I can't determine if you're joking or serious. That's worrisome."

"Well it wasn't exactly the Ghost of Christmas Past, but I think he's linked to that music box. He seems to have an interest in it."

Madeleine's eyebrows were practically hovering over her head at this point. "It seems you have quite the relationship with... *him* already. Why are we just hearing about this now?"

"Because it sounds crazy and I don't know what he wants."

"We're past crazy. We solved a murder with the help of ghosts, remember?" Ro said.

"I wonder what he wants with the music box?" Lucy mused.

"I don't know but I need a spell to keep him out of my bedroom, that scared me and the cats too much."

Lucy's eyes were round, "is that something we can do?"

"Uh." I had meant it as a joke.

Ro snorted. "Listen, accepting ghosts is hard enough. I do *not* believe in magic."

"Well," Madeleine began.

"Not. Magic." Ro enunciated each word.

Madeleine threw her a disgruntled look.

"Let's talk about this after we help Lucy finish getting this place ready for customers." I hadn't meant to take so much time away from her.

Madeleine narrowed her eyes at me. "You told me earlier that you weren't a verb but from now on if I ever see another ghost or dead body I'm saying that I was Cammie'd."

I restrained myself from tossing a breadstick at her. It would be a waste of a good breadstick.

"I want to see that music box again." Ro said, grabbing another box and prying it open to reveal decor for the shop.

Soothing canvas prints of various flowers, foliage, and nature, including an adorable bee one, were soon hanging on the walls, giving the place a relaxed feel.

Two hours later we had finished organizing and arranging what she had for the moment.

"What kind of furniture are you getting?" I asked. We had set up many elegant shelves on the walls along with the canvas artwork and the place was decorated beautifully, with colorful, ornate rugs covering the floor. Christmas decorations were up along with the regular decor of her new shop, replete with a pair of snowmen, each with big lashes and big smiles on their faces, waving their mittened hands.

"I have the cutest reading cubbies for kids, they're in diamond shapes and stacked on top of one another so kids can hang out while their parents are browsing. Then I'll get small tables and comfy chairs. Maybe a couch, I'm envisioning it over there." she pointed toward the other side of the room. "The bookshelves I'm getting are mahogany and will work nicely with the floor, I think. The snack bar will go there, it won't be too much but just a little something for people to nibble on while they read or take with them on the road. I'll also have some of Bianca's flowers on display for sale in a glass refrigerator over here, and on the displays we just put together I'm going to put mugs and book trinkets like magnetic bookmarks for sale." She lit up when she spoke, gesturing as she painted the lovely bustling image of what the shop would be in our minds. I was so excited for her, if anyone could make this work, she could.

"This is wonderful Lucy." Ro said, as earnest as I've ever seen her. "I can't wait to see the finished shop."

"Our town is lucky." Madeleine agreed.

We finished up and then went our separate ways. I would be at the children's toy drive mid-morning tomorrow so after carefully checking my closet and room for floating intruders, I changed into my pajamas and went to bed. Hopefully no ghosts would disturb my sleep tonight.

Chapter 8

The toy drive was bustling with people and of course the main gossip was the parade. Several ladies to the left of me were chattering about it, sharing tidbits that they had heard.

"Well good riddance I say. No one liked the man. Did you see him and our city attorney Anthony Blake get into it that one day?" the lady with a long black wool coat and a chihuahua held in one arm said.

"That's nothing compared to what I heard Charles say about him. Even his daughter hates the man." the woman with a leather purse the size of a suitcase emphasized.

"Small towns, eh?" A lady in front of me said. A minute ago I had given her the card to fill out with information and told her where to put the toys she brought.

"Gives them something to do I guess." My curiosity peaked. "Did you know him?"

She paused her writing and gave a humorless laugh. "I worked with him."

"Oh." I refrained from asking if he was as bad as everyone made him sound. Barely.

Apparently my ability to filter my work words did not translate to my expressions as she gave a little half smile and said, "yes he was an awful person." she glanced around then looked back at me. "I'll tell you the truth, whoever offed him did the world a favor."

"It's hard to imagine someone that bad." I said nonchalantly, hoping that she would expound.

She scoffed. "He was a bully, a pathological liar, and was always into some new business deal using other people's money. And let me tell you, it didn't always go well. A man named Charles sunk the money he was saving for his daughter's college into a business that looked good on paper but was in fact, not real. His poor daughter. He conned her dad into spending her budding college fund on a business venture that of course went nowhere. The least he could have done would be to target people who didn't have children. I saw her at the parade that day around the time Darwin bit the dust, but I didn't see him besides when he was on the float. He played Santa."

I blinked, they'd said they'd been together at the time of the murder. Maybe that wasn't true.

"There were a lot of people dressed up like elves, maybe they were actually together. What did you say his last name was?"

"No, it was definitely her. She was behind the ice sculptures right before Darwin was killed. And, it's Lodus. Anyway, thank you for the help." She handed me the document. Her name was Kylie.

I made a mental note of her name and the odd discrepancy she provided. The ice sculptures were close to the back entrance of Santa's Workshop.

Shaking off the errant thoughts I continued to help people sign up and direct them to where they could deposit their toys. Toys that weren't in packaging, such as stuffed animals, I had people place in a clear plastic bag before they joined the other toys. I was particularly excited when the ladies of the church women's group came carrying loads of books. They had books for small children all the way up to upper teens. I was thrilled. I thought I was the only one who had brought books. Of course I also brought other toys as well but it was especially important for children who maybe didn't have as much to be able to learn to read well and also to escape into the worlds of fiction books.

MILK, COOKIES, AND MURDER

It was mid-afternoon when we started cleaning up and packing things away into the suburban headed for the city where they would hand off the toys to social workers.

I spent another hour engaged in conversation and laughter with the other volunteers as we had cider, hot chocolate, and sandwiches as a thank you for our help.

At home I cleaned the house, played with the kitties, and prepped dinner. I usually like my alone time but right now I missed Gavin.

The cats crowded me as I sat down on the couch with my dinner. "Get off me you fiends. You already ate."

I tucked in with a book after dinner and didn't pull my nose out of it until my phone started going off.

I snatched the phone from the coffee table. "Hello?"

"Cammie!" Lucy's voice was high pitched and desperate.

"What's going on sweetie?" I pushed my book to the side and focused on her. She was not usually one for hysterics. That was Madeleine's job.

She started crying and then after a moment of burbling someone else took the phone.

"They arrested Santa." Ro said dryly. "He's been accused of the murder."

Santa...Oh no. "Charles has been arrested?"

"His daughter is here and asking for Lucy's help since she knows Lucy was involved with what happened with the pile of bones you found."

"Alan Garrett!" pile of bones was just too callous for me. "What do you want me to do?" there was nothing I could do about this.

"Come chat with us. Help this kid understand what the process is going to look like."

"And maybe help prove that her dad didn't do anything." Lucy finally managed to get in. She must have wrestled the phone back.

I didn't know about that. He was as good a guess as any, especially with what Darwin's colleague had said at the toy drive.

"Okay, where are you?"

"At the shop." Ro said it so easily and if the circumstances were different I would have smiled. I had a feeling that it would soon become an often frequented and well loved spot by all of us.

I sobered quickly. "I'll be down. But you know there's nothing I can do." I wasn't sure at all what I would say to a kid whose dad just got arrested. Did she have anyone besides him?

"Thanks."

I said bye and hung up.

My cat meowed at me, disgruntled, as I gently pushed him off my lap and got up. "Don't fuss at me, mister. You never cared all that much about laying on my lap until we had another cat in the house. Jealousy does not look good on you, even if your eyes are a lovely green."

I pulled on a sweater and wool coat and headed out into the night. The darkness accented the beauty that was the neighborhood. Rows of cottage homes decorated with icicle lights, soft white lights, big red bows lined with colored lights decorating fence posts, and some with decorated Christmas trees in their yards, it all came alive in the darkness. I took a moment to breathe in the cool air and enjoy the brilliant shine against the darkening, blue black background.

I got in my car and headed over to the shop.

Everyone was there. Jenny was sitting with Lucy, her under eyes dark from grief or lack of sleep. Probably both.

Madeleine Seemed more resigned than usual and I went over to her first.

"I'm not sure what we're supposed to do." I said.

She shook her head. "There's nothing we can do. But what a horrible thing to happen to that child."

I went over to Lucy, wondering why Ro hadn't just told them the truth of the matter. We couldn't do anything to help. We didn't have the resources or knowledge and it wasn't impossible for her father to have done it. Ro was always a straightforward one, sometimes taking it to the point of harshness. But today she wasn't saying anything. She did look very uncomfortable though.

"Oh good." she said when I came over, standing up and waving me toward the chair with both hands as if she couldn't get away fast enough. Dealing with emotions was not her strong suit.

"Hi Lucy, hey Jenny." I sat in the seat Ro had so aggressively gestured at is she not so subtly took a chair a ways from us.

Jenny looked up and met my gaze with crystal blue ones that tore into me and making me feel guilty. "I remember it was in the paper that you helped solve a murder only a few months ago."

I took a breath, trying to figure out what I should say to that, but when I opened my mouth she quickly continued.

"My dad wouldn't hurt anybody. He wouldn't do anything to leave me. Will you help me find the real killer so he doesn't stay in jail?"

"That was a completely different circumstance, I'm not an investigator or anything. The police are the ones tasked with gathering evidence of who did it."

"From listening to chief Papasadoris, this case is solved." Lucy's eyes flashed with anger.

Of course, why was I not surprised.

"Still, that doesn't mean we can do anything helpful."

Jenny started tearing up, "please give my dad a chance. He's a good person. He works so hard and he's taken such good care of me since mom died." A little sob tore through her and then Lucy started crying.

As Lucy held her, both of them crying, I put my face in my hands. How could I say no to her request? But what if it was her father? Telling her that would be devastating as well.

A hand gently pressed on my shoulder and I looked up. Madeleine met my gaze somberly. "You're not alone in this. I'll help too. For the sake of this child."

Ro was nodding despite her earlier hesitation. "She deserves to know the truth." She looked at me and Madeleine and then Lucy, "whatever it may be."

I turned to Jenny, still cuddled up next to Lucy, looking much younger than her years with her puffy red eyes and quivering lips. Lucy was rubbing her shoulder soothingly.

"Jenny, I can't promise that your dad didn't do it. But we will look into it, okay?"

"Thank you." her voice was soft and small and she seemed so alone. I would do what I needed to find out what happened so she had some closure.

"But that means there can't be any secrets between us. I know you weren't with your dad so he doesn't have you as in alibi. Where was he when you last saw him and where were you?" I saw her expression and explained, "we need to be able to see a clear picture of where everyone was and what was happening. If you keep things from us we can't form that picture and might not be able to find what was really going on as easily."

She nodded and wiped the tears away with the backs of her hands. "I hated him. He treated dad so badly. He even took money away from us. And then he laughed about it. So when I saw him at the parade I got so angry. He shouldn't have been able to enjoy it when he was such an awful person. So I followed him to talk to him." she sniffled and shrugged "yell at him, I guess. Tell him to give my dad back the money. Dad was playing his role as Santa when I left. I followed that awful man but then he disappeared in the building. I guess it was because he'd put on that costume."

"Do you have any idea why he would put on a costume?" I asked. I had little hope that she knew but anything could help.

She shook her head. "I have no idea. He was in normal clothes when he was at the parade."

I took a mental note. He'd changed quite quickly before going out among the crowd again.

"A disguise." Ro said.

I nodded my agreement. "Yes but the question is why? Someone was there that he didn't want to see him."

"Or they'd seen him and he wanted to get away from them." Madeleine said.

True, he might have known that someone was out to murder him.

I glanced at Jenny. "Do you have someone to stay with?" Wouldn't social services be involved if she didn't? I had no idea how this went.

"My grandma came here but she has a caretaker and has a lot of problems that keep her caretaker busy." She held back more tears but the pain must have been immense. She didn't truly have anyone, and I wondered if they even noticed that she was gone.

I gave her the best reassuring smile I could. "Again I can't promise you anything but we're going to make a plan and see what we can find out. Your job in all this is to go home and continue in your routine is much as possible. Okay?"

She opened her mouth as though she didn't want to agree to what I said, then closed it and nodded, clearly too tired to argue. I doubt she'd been sleeping much these days.

"I'll drive you home." Lucy said.

"What's the first step?" Madeleine asked.

I smiled. "What we do best, dig into history. I want to find out if Darwin Lodus has ever been married or sued. And if not then I'm going to find his girlfriend."

Ro was nodding. "Guys like that always have someone they've manipulated to date them."

"I'll let you know what I find out tomorrow." Now all I wanted was to just crawl into bed.

The next day I easily found out that Darwin had an ex-wife and that it happened to be Mandy, the real estate agent. Yes, I could see her having a bad taste in men. Luckily though her office wasn't far away so I walked over there on my lunch break.

I'd had an extra cup of coffee today in order to help me be more talkative and outgoing. Goodness knows I would just rather curl up with a good book or talk to one or two people about history. Hoping it energized me enough I walked up to the counter and chatted with the receptionist who walked me back to Mandy's office.

"Hello!" she greeted me enthusiastically.

Smiling, I handed her a tin of fudge that I had made. "I hope I'm not bothering you, I just wanted to go around and chat with people and give them desserts, showing my appreciation for them." It wasn't a lie, I would be taking fudge to anyone else I talked to. People couldn't be mean to someone who gave them fudge, right?

"That's so nice! Why don't you have a seat, let's chat."

For the next several minutes *we* did not chat, she chatted while I wondered how to bring up my topic naturally. I didn't need to worry because inevitably she started talking about the parade and what had happened. "I'm his ex-wife you know. He made me really think he loved me in the beginning. He was a good liar. He got off on ripping people off. I really hope they're lenient on that banker." She said.

"It sounded like there was a lot of people who disliked him." I said, using what Ro had told me was an elicitation technique where instead of asking a question you made a statement that would get people talking. Usually it was a statement that they needed to disprove which would then cause them to expound because people liked explaining things to others and had a need to be right.

"Ugh," She gave me a look, "don't even get me started. He always had these schemes to make money and he was really good at talking people into investing in them. But he was never as smart as he thought and he lost so much money. So much." she rolled her eyes, flicking her manicured nails as she spoke. I hadn't noticed that they were shaped like spears until then. How women managed to grab things, type on computers, use their phone and do daily life like cleaning with pointy, two inch long nails was beyond me. "He even" she widened her eyes for emphasis, "had a black and blue bruise on his face the last time I saw him."

"What?" and I wasn't even acting when my mouth dropped open.

She nodded vigorously, clearly excited that she'd gotten a strong reaction to what she said. She continued on. "He said his girlfriend did it, which made it so much better. He was so mad that I laughed." At my surprised gaze she shook her head and chuckled, "you don't realize what an awful man he is. Was."

I swallowed, "do you think the banker really did it? With all these other people who don't like him? His own girlfriend even smacked him, that's violent."

She leaned forward, "I hadn't even thought of that. But the police seemed to think it's him."

"From what I've heard they don't have a lot of evidence."

She was clearly excited to have the juicy information. I just needed two more questions answered before I left.

"Is she also in real estate? Maybe I'd recognize her name."

"Oh goodness no!" she frowned and shook her head. "I've had some competition come into town recently but certainly not her. She's a paralegal. Her name is Cinda. I doubt you know her, she's fairly new to the area. She's only been here about a year. He couldn't get anyone who's lived here for a while to date him because we all have his number now." She curled her lip.

"I see." I couldn't show her that I was excited at the information. Things were so much more efficient when people lived in a small town and knew what other people were up to. "Anyway, back to better things. The floats on display in the parade were absolutely stunning, don't you think?"

"It's always so beautiful but I had to miss it this year."

"Oh no, that's unfortunate. I hope everything's alright."

She waved a hand dismissively. "I was at home sick is all."

Hmm. So no one to verify where she was.

She walked me out, chattering happily about the Christmas decorations and how much she loved the cold weather. Madeleine would scold her.

Back at work I took a look at the newspaper. Darwin's work had made a statement, showcasing a picture of his boss and coworkers as they expressed their sadness at losing a colleague. Hmm. I studied the image. The boss, three men and a receptionist. I didn't see the lady who said she was his colleague.

I turned my attention back to my computer and found an e-mail waiting from Ro, CCing the other ladies, asking if I had brought the music box to work. In truth I'd been so distracted by the other events that I hadn't thought to grab it this morning. I wrote back and asked if anyone wanted to see it at my house after work.

Lucy was the first to write back, with a *yes!*

Emails from Madeleine and Ro conveyed their agreement and Ro offered to bring dinner.

Will it be healthy food? I typed, just to tease her. She had always let loose during Christmas and on birthdays but that was it and seeing it as it was Christmastime she probably wouldn't try to get us to drink disgusting green smoothies and eat veggies with hummus.

Most certainly. She typed back. I could just see her smirk.

The ladies arrived not long after I got home and I left the door open for them.

Ro opened the back door to her car and delicious smells wafted to me. I'm kicked out of my slippers and pulled on a pair of boots so I could go down and help her. It looked like she'd gotten both a tray of lasagna as well as chicken alfredo. My stomach rumbled appreciatively.

"If this is what healthy is, I'm in." I said, grinning.

She laughed as she took the first tray up the steps and into the house.

"Cammie?" She called from inside.

"Yes?" I answered, pulling the last tray from the car.

"Either there are ghost cats that we can now see or you have a trespasser." She said.

"That's just Holly. She's staying with us over the holidays until she can get adopted."

"Is it weird that I'm disappointed that it's not a ghost cat?" Lucy asked.

"No." Ro spoke the same time that Madeleine said, "yes."

Lucy looked at me, her face holding a long-suffering expression. I shrugged. "Don't look at me, i have no comment."

We hustled to get everything dished out and onto the Christmas plates that I pulled out from storage, as I did every year. They had various designs, a red barn behind a decorated tree with a snowman waving from behind another tree; a deer draped in lights with decorated Christmas trees in the background; a snowman with a black top hat and red scarf with a squirrel sitting at his side, looking up at him, and a brilliant red Christmas cardinal sitting on one of his branch arms. I found the images to be both beautiful and peaceful.

I pulled the music box out, setting it on the central coffee table in front of us all. We settled on my loveseat and two plush chairs in the living room and I got them up to speed about the research I'd done on the music box as we ate.

When I was finished with my explanation, which I tried to keep short and failed, I asked, "So what do you think?" I hoped they had some ideas that could help me discover the true origin of this ornate box.

"I think that we should sell it and get a ton of money for it." Ro said.

"I wonder why there would be a ghost looking after that particular music box?" Lucy frowned into space as she twirled the linguine around her fork.

"You know what I wonder?" Madeleine's eyes lit up and she flashed a playful grin. "If you've gone on a date with Mr. tall dark and available."

I threw my head back and laughed at the horrified look on Lucy's face, even as she flushed to her roots.

"You ladies are awful." She said, but a smile was playing on her lips and her eyes lit up.

"I think we have our answer," I said.

"I'm kind of hurt you didn't tell us about it." Madeliene said.

Lucy waved her hands, "no, no. It's not like that. He just asked me and we're meeting this weekend. Believe me, you'll get to hear all about it, good or bad."

"It better be good or we might have to mug him." Ro said.

I was about to expound on what a horrible idea it would be to mug a cop, and couldn't we think of a less violent way to deal with him if he's not to Lucy's standards, when suddenly the cats raced out of the room like they'd just seen a ghost.

What…Oh no.

All our gazes drifted over to the see-through man dressed in that classy old suit floating just above the floor as he looked down at the music box. I held my breath and felt the others do the same. He looked at each of us, meeting our gazes, and then down at the box. Then he looked back at me and back down to the box where he let his gaze linger for a moment before he vanished.

After a few seconds of silence Lucy's shaky voice sounded, "he seems like a very polite ghost."

I chuckled nervously.

"Do you think this was his music box? That he made it or owned it?" Madeleine narrowed her eyes at the box as though it would help her see into its past.

MILK, COOKIES, AND MURDER

"It's probable." I couldn't help but reach over and pick it up again. It was very big for a music box, very solid. Was it all solid? I touched around it. No part of it seemed different or amiss.

"Then he probably wants it on his grave or with him?" Lucy wrinkled her brow at that.

Ro sniffed derisively at that. "They're hardly going to let us exhume a body just to put a music box in with it."

"I agree on both counts, and if we find out who it belongs to we can just go and put it on his grave. No exhumation necessary." I hoped that was all that was needed to get rid of the so far nice but startling ghost.

We discussed different ways that we could find the owner.

"A lot of times people are known for their own specific details or unique way they do something." Madeleine suggested.

"You're right," I snapped my fingers, "often they also embed their signature." We all gathered close as I lifted the box so we could examine It. I'd looked before, but it wouldn't hurt to look again. We looked over every square centimeter. Nothing.

"Wait, turn it over again." Lucy said.

I did as she asked.

She narrowed her eyes then smiled. "There." She pointed.

On the bottom on the back rim, so faded and small I could barely make them out, were the initials VT.

"That's a boatload of help." Ro said.

"It's better than nothing." Lucy said.

After a few more minutes of discussing what we could do next to try and find out more about the box, we determined that Ro would drive up to Chesterton and take it to a professional in an antique business to see what they had to say and if there was anything about the box that could be traced back.

"Did you find anything out about Darwin?" Lucy changed the subject, gaze on me.

"I found that he has an ex-wife in town and I went to talk to her."

"Who is that?" Madeleine asked.

"Mandy Bunk."

"The realtor?" Lucy squeaked.

"I knew that hussy had bad taste." Madeleine shook her head.

Lucy rolled her eyes at Madeleine's judgment.

"What did she say?" Ro asked, getting us back on track.

"She said his girlfriend gave him a black eye."

"I knew it! It's always the significant other." Madeleine nodded as if the whole thing had been solved.

If only it were that simple. "I'm going to see her either tomorrow or the next day whenever I can get out. And then this Friday Ro will be taking the box up to Chesterton to have it looked at, so hopefully that will prove useful." I turned to her. "Thank you again for doing that. I'll be too busy with that family gathering to take it when I'm there."

"Hopefully this will be a fun time for you guys." Lucy said, probably seeing the wince I made when I mentioned my family and tried to be upbeat about it.

"I really hope so, it would be nice to make some more good memories."

Ro eyebrows shot up, "more?"

"I have some good memories with them." I defended. When she didn't stop staring at me, eyebrow quirked, waiting for me to expound, I blew out a breath. "There have been a few, I just can't think of them."

No one pushed.

"You have your in-laws here, how are they?" I turned to Madeleine.

She lifted her gaze to the ceiling, "please don't remind me."

"It can't be that bad." I encouraged.

She gave me a look that had been similar to Ro's. OK then maybe it could be.

"We're here for you." Lucy said encouragingly.

We talked some more about the murder, family plans, and the music box.

"This sure is wrapping up to be a busy month." Madeleine looked at the fruit cocktail she'd poured herself, "I should have brought wine."

"What can I do to help you with looking into the situation for Jenny and Charles?" Lucy asked. Her expression turned hopeful. "Charles should be out on bail soon, so you'll be able to talk to him as well."

"That will be helpful, and you don't need to do anything. You're already doing enough by spending time with Jenny and helping around their house while her grandmother is the one taking care of her."

"Taking care of." Madeleine said with a skeptical look.

I continued, ignoring the sadness I felt for Jenny. She didn't even have proper care while her dad was in jail. And during Christmas, especially. "Plus, you have a new shop you're getting set up and all the planning and paperwork that goes with it."

"That's right, do you need any more help with all that?" Ro asked.

"Actually this weekend the furniture is going to be all delivered along with the last boxes of everything—if the shipment is on time—so if you would help me put the rest of the items away and move furniture around, that would be amazing." She waved her hands in front of her, "of course that's if you have time."

"We always have time for you." Madeleine said. I nodded my firm agreement.

I promised to let them know how it went with the girlfriend and they said they would look into a few angles on their end. Mainly that meant that Madeleine and Lucy would do some digging on Charles because we had to know if we were barking up the wrong tree and it really was him. If we didn't make sure we could just be running in circles trying to look at others who had motive. Because, as Ro said, he had motive, means, and opportunity, so he needed to be ruled out once and for all.

We say goodnight and Ro took the box with her. I went to my bedroom to change and get in bed with a book, but first I looked around, checking to make sure that the ghost had indeed went with the box. Not that I knew that for sure but he wasn't in my house now at the very least.

I looked at the cats who were gazing at me from the bed on opposite sides. Clearly they still weren't best friends. "At least we shouldn't have any more scary visitors tonight." I assured them, hoping I was right.

Chapter 9

There were two other full legal services in town besides the city attorney, who, if their hostile exchange at the craft fair was any indication, also had reason to hate that man. I needed to talk with him as well. Not that I thought Mr. Blake did it, but rather, I wanted his take on the whole thing.

The first law office did not have a Cinda working there so I made my way to the second one. The business was housed in a cute, cottage style building that had two businesses in it, one upstairs and one down. The legal office was downstairs.

"Hi, does Cinda work here?" I asked as I walked into the small lobby area.

The woman at the desk beamed, "yep that's me!" She stood from her seat at the computer so she could properly see me over the front desk.

"Hi. I wanted to bring these to you for condolences." I handed her some fudge.

Her eyes went round as she accepted the tin and peered inside, "oh this looks delicious. But I don't understand, why you're giving it to me?"

"Oh, I'm sorry. I thought it was your significant other who tragically lost his life at the parade." Gavin would be so excited at my deviousness these days.

"Yes, it was very sad." she said without a shred of said sadness on her face.

"Were you happy?" I bit the inside of my cheek at the very blatant invasion of privacy. Thankfully, she didn't seem to mind.

"I'll admit, I left him over a week ago. He was just such a..." She didn't continue instead giving me a fake smile, "I just hope he rests in peace."

"Of course. It's just such a tragedy. Who do you think could have done something like that?"

"Ugh, a whole number of people." she pursed her lips, "he was a real jerk sometimes."

"That's why you did what was best for you and broke up with him." I said with sympathy in my eyes. I meant it, sometimes awful guys could be very charming and drew unknowing ladies in before they showed their real character.

She nodded, "I found out he was seeing someone in the city when he went up there on his so-called business trips. How shocking." She looked disgusted.

"How could he? What an awful man. Did you see him when you were at the parade?"

"No, I didn't get to see the whole parade this year."

"Oh that's too bad. It's such a fun event to miss."

"I know. My sisters drove down to attend but my grandma had a stroke so we left early." she admitted.

"That's horrible, I'm so sorry. Is she okay?"

"It's not as bad as it could have been, she's still recovering from it, but so far it looks like she's recovering well. Thank you for asking."

I smiled and reached out to squeeze her hand comfortingly. "Give her my well wishes when you see her next."

She smiled back, a real smile this time with her eyes crinkling. "I will and thank you for the fudge."

"Of course!" I started to turn. "I should let you get back to work." Wait, one more thing. I turned back. "Were your sisters with you for the whole time you were at the parade?"

"Yes."

"What was their favorite float?" I asked it because I was curious and it would also tell me that she wasn't lying.

She named it and then said the one she thought was the best as well.

"Of course, we didn't get to see them all." She paused. "I hope you don't think I sound crass when talking about Darwin. He was just not a very nice person but I am really sad that he's gone." Suddenly something seemed to come to mind. "A couple of weeks ago Victor Tjernagel smashed Darwin's windshield with a shovel. For whatever reason he never told the police. That was the type of person he was though, always getting on people's bad side."

My eyes popped open. Well that was violent. I wouldn't have ever thought that old man was strong enough to kill him, but if he'd managed to smash his car...

"And you have no idea what he did that made Mr. Tjernagel become so angry?"

She rolled her eyes, "it's not hard to make Victor angry. He's a grumpy old man, that's for sure."

"Quite cantankerous." I agreed. I had a feeling I wouldn't get any more helpful information out of her. "Thank you."

We said bye and I headed out. Talking to Victor would be easier said than done.

I went back to work to finish out the day. I called Ro to ask about an archive the library might have that we didn't but was informed by her co-worker that she had been sick.

Ro never got sick so I dialed her. No answer, she was probably sleeping. I would check on her later.

Madeleine called me to report that she hadn't been able to find out anything about a woodworker from the friends that she had who had been here for decades or had family that had been here for generations.

She changed the subject. "If I'm honest with you I have my reservations about this whole getting involved in the murder bit, but it does seem strange to me the more that I hear about it. What was Charles' motive? What happened between them was over a year ago. He'd finally just started to recover the money and refill his daughter's college account. There's no reason he would have been angry enough to kill him *now*. It wasn't in the time frame of a passion killing like it would be if it was when he had just lost the money."

I frowned. That was good to know. "Thank you for telling me that, and you're right, it doesn't add up. After he makes bail and spends a few days with his daughter we should go talk to him."

"He would likely feel safest at the shop with Lucy instead of his house or one of ours. Neutral ground so to speak."

"If she's okay with that, I think that's a good idea." At this rate Lucy's shop was just going to become a bookshop slash counseling center slash investigation room.

After work I headed to the store. I would never hear the end of it if I went to Ro's house to make sure she wasn't dead, but if I made her soup and got her some other goodies she wouldn't fuss so much.

I texted her so she knew I was coming, then drove over to her house. She was at the window and held up a hand in greeting while I dropped off the basket and canister of soup.

Doing okay? I texted, then looked back at her.

She looked down, then back up and nodded. My phone chimed. *Just tired.*

I left for the warmth of my home and hoped she felt better soon. I had a feeling she'd have company while she recovered since she had the music box.

Saturday afternoon rolled around after a busy week and I found myself at the burgeoning bookshop. Men carried in furniture from the big box truck parked out front. They were fairly indiscriminate in where they put the furniture even as Lucy rushed around squawking like a chicken and waving her hands here and there, trying to get them to place the heavy pieces at least in the vicinity of where they needed to be so that we could easily move them to be positioned how she wanted them. Pride blossomed on my face, this was good for her. Even if she did look a bit stressed with her hair sticking to her sweating face.

The men finished hauling everything in and left unceremoniously, leaving the door open. Jenny set at a table that had been set up earlier while Lucy spun in a circle with her hands on her hips frowning.

"At least they got them on the right sides of the room." she said before glancing at me. "Would you help me shove them into the positions I want them to have?"

"Of course. Those things don't stand a chance of not moving when I throw my hips against them." I winked.

My bravado was short lived as we tried to get a coffee colored full leather couch exactly where she wanted it.

"We're almost there." she coached. We'd put a blanket underneath it so we could slide it better and not scratch the floor. It had worked better in my mind than it did in reality.

"And you said this would be easy." she panted. "You're not walking the walk, Cammie." she joked.

"Oh, I can walk the walk. Just don't ask me to jog the jog or run the run which has the same effect on my lungs as trying to move this thing around. Couldn't you have bought lighter furniture?"

"I didn't think one hundred and sixty pounds would be so heavy."

"Excuse me."

So caught up in our own little world we both jumped and yelped at the masculine voice. Lucas stood at the door with a look of humor in his eyes.

My hand went to my heart as Lucy smiled and brush the hair away from her face, "Lucas, how are you?"

"Doing better than you two, it seems. I was going to walk by and not bother you but you're moving that couch so slowly that you're not going to be finished getting it where you want it by the time our date rolls around, so I thought I'd help."

Luby's cheeks flamed and I stifled a laugh.

"I should reject your offer just because of that remark." she said primly, nose tilted in the air in faux arrogance while her eyes sparkled. "But I'm already exhausted and willing to be humble if it means I don't have to spend another half hour trying to get this thing where I want it."

"Fair enough." he strode in, waved us away from it, and maneuvered it as Lucy instructed.

"I want it over there, no just a little bit to the left, that's it, now back a little bit further, I want it diagonal."

No wonder we hadn't gotten very far, she was terrible at giving directions. I'm pretty sure she changed her mind at least four times in the span of the next few minutes.

"Lucy if you didn't really know where you wanted it why did we start moving it in the first place?" I said.

She side-eyed me with a little smile playing on her lips. "It needs to be just right and I don't know exactly what that looks like until it's in this area I want it to be in."

"Uh-huh."

I wandered over to sit by Jenny. She was playing some game on a tablet. Her elbow was resting on the table, her face scrunched against her fist while she played with the other hand. She didn't look at all happy or even remotely distracted by the game.

I was tempted to say something such as 'how are you holding up?' But what kind of a foolish question was that? I knew how she was doing, I could see it in the dark circles and pinched lines of her face.

"Your dad should be getting out on bail soon. You must be happy."

"My dad didn't do anything wrong but he'll have to go back."

Couldn't argue with that. "Have you been going to any of the Christmas events around town?" At least it might get her mind off of the situation.

"Lucy takes me to things when she can. And so does my teacher Mrs. Green." Where once her eyes glittered with life and excitement they were now dull as she lifted them to meet my gaze. "Were you able to find anything to help my dad?"

"I have been talking to people." I promised. "So far there's nothing promising yet." I wasn't about to tell her about Victor Tjernagel. He might have been angry but that didn't make him a killer.

I stayed with Jenny until Lucy and Lucas were done with their rearranging. When they'd finished and moved their attention to us, I stood. "I'm off now, I have to get ready to head to Chesterton this afternoon. Enjoy your date." I turned my eyes to the girl again. Shoulders hunched, never moving her cheek from her fist as she stared down. "Do you want me to drop Jenny off at her house on my way home?"

Lucy gazed sadly at her then shook her head, "no, I will. Thank you though."

At home I had to shake myself from the melancholy of what was going on and got everything ready. I wanted to see family again and even if I didn't, they were expecting me and I should show up.

The theme of this party was the Twelve Days of Christmas. I wanted to know who had decided on that. If it'd been put to a vote I hadn't been included. Still, in the spirit of being an enthusiastic part of the party, I had gotten a red a-line swing dress that had two turtle doves embroidered on the flaring skirt. I grabbed a white shawl to pull over it since it was short sleeved and as beautiful as I thought this time of year was with the sparkling white snow and fun decorations, I knew I would be cold without my coat, even inside.

I fed the cats before leaving and made sure the small cat fountain was full of water since I'd be staying the night in the city with mother.

Two and a half hours later I was at my great uncle Hendry's house. As I parked the car and looked at the house I wondered, not for the first time, why my family insisted on being house poor. The house must have at least been four thousand square feet. And he didn't have young children who needed the space. Oh well, at least it was good for entertaining the family during our holiday parties and other family events.

I hurried inside, the cold stinging my cheeks. The temperature had dropped rapidly and I shivered at the bone chilling wind. I rapped on the door and it only took a moment for someone to answer. That teenager I had spoken to at the previous family event, who used words I didn't understand and had to look up in on the internet, opened to the door.

"Hi." I greeted with a smile.

She gave me a little smile and stepped aside so I could get in and hang my coat up. This time I wasn't the last one there, giving me an opportunity to actually go and talk to more people since groups weren't already set in deep conversation.

"Doug so good to see you." I greeted my uncle. He was a short man with wisps of white hair and kind brown eyes. I had to stop myself from laughing at his outfit. He wore regular clothes, and over them he had placed an apron decorated with hens.

"Cammie!" he greeted me with a hug. "We didn't get to chat last time, pull up a chair and tell me what's been going on."

We got to talking. Doug had retired and now spent his days giving golf lessons since he loved the sport so much. We talked about the recent uptick in younger people joining golf and how it was a technical sport despite what some people thought of it. Me, I was that some people. But I didn't admit it. Then our conversation rolled around to the historical society and I also told him about the events at the parade.

"What a horrible thing for you to experience!" he said, aghast. Clearly he hadn't been told about my other misadventure earlier this year. Best kept that way. I told him about the different suspects.

I leaned closer, lowering my voice, "who do you think did it?" It was more of a question of humor than me truly wondering. It would give him something to think about and maybe he would come up with something that would be helpful.

His face lit up at being asked. "Well, I think that it must be a crime of passion. If someone was plotting against him because he'd wronged them in the past, it wouldn't have been so messy. He wouldn't have been stumbling out among a huge crowd of people."

My brows went up, that was a good thought. "You're right! It had to be someone he'd hurt very recently or even in the moment."

"Are you sure you heard that both the ex-wife and the ex-girlfriend have solid alibis? I would look into that angle if I were the police." I hadn't told him I was actually looking into it, just that I knew about it.

I glanced up from our conversation and made eye contact with my mom heading toward us from across the expansive room.

"You didn't even come say hi." My mother made her way up to us.

I stood and gave her a hug, "sorry, Doug and I were deep in an interesting conversation."

She raised her eyebrows, "oh, what about?"

"She was telling me about a murder that happened in her town during the parade." Doug supplied. I winced, wishing he had mentioned something about the historical society or golf instead.

Her eyebrows lowered and she gave me a disapproving look. "That's not a polite topic of conversation. Certainly not for a Christmas party."

"I thought it was rather interesting." Doug said. Mom leveled her quelling glare from me to him.

He waved his hands in surrender. "I guess I'll go talk to someone else about golf, it's a technical sport you know." he said humorously.

By this time the large space had filled up with family. Gavin's sister was sitting on the couch diagonal to me fanning herself and getting a foot massage by one of our aunts. People say that there's a pregnancy glow but all I saw was a very uncomfortable woman. She wasn't that pregnant though, only five months.

As I watched she leaned her head back and closed her eyes, "would someone get me some water? A cookie would be nice too." Her mom, nearby, hurried off to get them for her.

Someone clapped their hands to get people's attention. "All right everybody," Hendry's wife, Lorinda, started loudly so she could be heard by everyone. "We're going to start playing some games and then we're going to give out a prize to whoever has the best costume. We'll all get a vote so take a look around and head over to that box," she pointed, "to cast your vote. One each." She said sternly as the teens hurried over.

I glanced around. Doug and myself were clearly underdressed for the theme. Uncle Jimmy had a full costume as a pear tree with a partridge sitting on it. Of course cousin Joan wore a dress with swans outlined in cubic zirconia decorating it. They sparkled every time she moved. It was very pretty, but I also felt that it was a bit overdone, this was a family get together not a fashion show. Everyone else had various outfits commemorating the twelve days.

Gavin's sister had just a dress on and when I asked she flared her arms out in what I assumed she thought was an elegant pose. "I'm a lady dancing."

I guess that worked.

"Everyone looks so lovely." Aunt Jennifer looked over at one of my cousins. "except for Ben, who did not dress up according to the theme."

"Eh hem," Ben cleared his throat purposefully and held up his left hand. 5 gold colored rings.

She laughed "I take that back."

I leaned toward Gavin who was sitting in the chair next to me, "he should have dressed as a lord and then gave a little hop saying he was one of the Lords a Leaping."

He laughed. "I don't know who came up with this theme," he whispered, "but next time I should get to choose."

I groaned. "I veto that, I don't have a dress for a masquerade ball."

Gavin burst out laughing again, "you have no faith in me."

"That is exactly right."

"I'm an excellent shopper, I would help you." He promised.

"I don't really love the idea of being dragged through clothing stores and made to show you fifty dresses on me until you decided that the first one was the best, three hours later." I grinned. He couldn't argue since he *had* dragged me through stores many times for long enough that my feet ached.

"Gavin, would you go get me some milk? That's what I want now." His sister said. She was in unusual form today. I noticed her husband wasn't here. Maybe they'd been fighting?

He glanced at her, then got up and went over to the kitchen. He came back and handed it to her. "Aren't pregnant ladies supposed to get a modicum of exercise?"

She huffed at him, not deigning to respond.

"Gavin be nice." His mother admonished.

Chelsey was an incredibly intelligent woman, and the pride of her family even though Gavin had built up his own thriving business on his own. They both had done well.

I got up and weaved my way through people to put in my vote. Gavin had worn a piper piping uniform, replete with a fake saxophone, kilt and white socks coming up to his knees. He by far was the most stylish of us all. It was in his DNA.

I made my way around the room, talking with family and listening to their vacation stories and who had bought a new house or car. We played games, and I got into a heated competition with my mom over Christmas bingo. We laughed. It was good to see everyone like this.

When it came time for the votes to be counted Lorinda stood at the front of the room and waved her hands dramatically. "And the winner is...Chelsey!"

People clapped and I focused on trying to keep my jaw from hitting the floor. She was just wearing a simple dress. Gavin was in a far more applicable outfit. Anyone else was wearing a far more applicable outfit. I understood that she was pregnant and she needed moral support, but treating her like she was a little child in need of constant bolstering and positive reinforcement grated on my nerves. Best not to think about it, it was just a simple thing, not worth getting worked up over. Still... I grabbed two cups of spiked punch and walked over to Gavin. He was having an interesting conversation with a teenager about some social media platform. He looked up and grinned when he saw what I had.

"Now that's what I'm talking about." he took the spiked punch and immediately began drinking.

"You look adorable. I voted for you." I muttered before taking a sip.

He shrugged and raised his eyebrows, "I won't be adding any children to the family tree so I bring an existential crisis where I could be passing on the family name." He was always so blasé about everything. He usually shrugged things off with a snarky comment, but I saw the flash of emptiness in his eyes. I knew it well because I felt it often. And I didn't have a sister competing for my parents' love. Not that people should have to compete for love.

I had noticed that while his mom hovered around his sister they hadn't spoken much. That I had paid attention to anyway.

"Cammie." Another cousin sidled up to me.

"Hi Dana."

"Come here and give me a squeeze, I haven't been able to chat with you yet." There was a reason for that. Dana was one of those people that was your best friend as soon as she started talking to you and the first to dive into the gossip about you when you weren't there. Ever since I'd been devastated over getting a C+ in one of my college science classes and she went around telling everyone that I wouldn't be able to finish my degree I'd spoken to her as little as possible. And honestly, I knew she didn't realize it was hurtful when she spread exaggerations about people. She wasn't purposefully malicious.

She looked past me after a quick hug. "Oooh, Gavin! Congratulations on your engagement."

I spun around and stared at him. His brows lowered for a brief moment as confusion flitted across his face, then mischief sparked in his eyes and lips quirked up.

"Thank you! You're going to be the ring bearer for me, right?"

"Uh, well..." Her face crinkled in bemusement.

"It's something important enough that I need to entrust it to someone like you."

"Of course then I'll help!" she started getting excited. "What's the color scheme?"

He glanced around, "red and green."

"Green?" She lifted an eyebrow daintily as if judging him but didn't say anything more.

He turned to me, "we're still on for the suit fitting, right?"

I dove in. "Absolutely. I think you really need to get those invitations out soon though, considering the wedding is in February." Then I went crazy. "Also, given that your sister-in-law was in that movie that became so popular, don't forget to hire the added security."

His eyes lit up, "that's right, she has that stalker!"

I looked at Dana, "but don't worry, we'll be safe. He only has one charge of running into a crowd and dancing around naked so I doubt it will happen again."

Dana's eyes bounced from me to Gavin like a pingpong ball, excitement shining on her face, her eyes wide. "While you two are discussing that I need to go say hi to a couple more people." And spread the story. So much for wanting to talk to me. She hurried away with a wave.

Gavin grinned.

"That was genius." I admired his quick and playful thinking. "You realize you're going to start shielding calls from everyone about this, right?"

"Gavin! Why didn't you tell me that you're getting married?" Uncle Doug marched over.

"That was fast." I muttered. "Bye!"

He gaped at me as I hurried away. This was a battle that was his to fight alone.

Grinning, I made my way over to grab a bite sized snack from one of the tiered trays.

My mother and one of my cousins came over.

"We haven't gotten to talk enough." My mother informed me.

"Well I will be spending the night at your house so I imagine we'll have some time to talk. If you're wondering why I didn't seek you out right away." Actually it wasn't that, it was the e-mail I'd gotten from her stating that she'd found an apartment she thought I would love, reminding me again that there was a nice man she wanted me to meet, and that she thought it was high time I stopped my nonsense and move back home.

"Your mom tells me that you're thinking about going back to school for a masters degree." My cousin Ben said.

My eyebrows flicked up in surprise. I had mentioned, briefly, in an effort to get her to understand how much I loved what I did, that I might go back to study further. That had been the end of that conversation.

"And it would be the perfect opportunity to come home and settle down now that you've sown your wild oats. You act too much like your father." My mother nodded along with her words as if she were agreeing with herself.

A little ball of ache settled in my chest. Bringing up dad, really? She's the one who chose him and married him and now she had to talk bad about him even to the grave. I didn't remember him well, but what memories I did have were of a man who liked to laugh and play with me.

"The masters degree idea was just something I was musing on. I love what I do and where I am. Mother I am in midlife now, you can stop trying to get me to conform."

"It's not conforming Cammie, it's living up to your potential and expectations. Ben here is going to get a masters already, at half your age. I want you to make the most of your life!"

I swallowed, trained to steady my emotions even as my heart slammed against my rib cage.

"Well Ben, you must be excited about what you do. Either that or you let people boss you around and make you do things that aren't worth your life. Because that's what this is, *your* one and only life. Excuse me."

I hurried away.

Gavin found me a few minutes later, sitting as far away from everyone else as I could. I'd pulled a book I kept permanently in my purse out and was trying to concentrate enough to get a page turned.

"Hey cuz." He flopped unceremoniously next to me, reminding me of when he was a lanky teenager. He leaned his head back on the couch. "The life has officially been sucked out of me." he said dramatically.

I mustered a smile, "then I must be talking to a ghost." He didn't seem to understand the humor I found in that sentence, nor would I ever tell him.

He looked at me, looked at the book, and then looked back at my face. He paused for a moment, then said, "what do you say you and I get out of here? There's this place I know that sells the absolute best pistachio ice cream. You've got to try it."

I glanced around the room. Family was congregated in different groups, playing games or talking. "Yes please."

Chapter 10

When I met the ladies at Lucy's shop that evening the next day Madeleine immediately peered at me. "Are you sick?"

"I wouldn't be here if I were sick. And I take offense that you think I look sick."

Lucy looked me over. "Rough day?"

I turned to Madeleine. "Your in laws should have been here long enough to have settled in, how's that going?"

She turned a thunderous scowl on me. "Don't even get me started."

"Really, don't get her started, you'll never be able to get her to stop." Ro chimed in helpfully from the storage room in the back.

Madeleine cast a glower in that direction then settled her gaze back on me. "Weren't you supposed to have a family party the other day?"

"Yep, that was last night." I dragged my coat off and proceeded to try to find something to work on. The place looked inviting, colorful and open, and most of the product she was selling had arrived.

"Do you want to talk about it?" Lucy asked.

I gave her a weak smile. "What I'd rather talk about is the murder. Or anything besides my family."

Ro came out from the back. "I'm sorry I've been out of the race. I wasn't able to get a lot done research wise on my end."

"Why on earth would you apologize? I remember seeing you through the window when I dropped off that soup. You looked like death."

She huffed a laugh, "I felt like it."

"Any new updates?" Lucy came to stand next to me, wringing her hands.

"So far the ex-girlfriend who gave him the black eye has an alibi, the ex-wife said she was home sick so no alibi, and the next person on my list is a grump I don't want to talk to."

"Should I go with you?" Ro asked.

"I'm going to procrastinate on that one and see if I can get something out of Attorney Blake. Seeing as I saw him arguing with the guy he definitely knows something about him. Maybe he has information that can help."

Madeleine sighed, "This isn't easy, everyone hated the guy."

"I wonder where the police are in their investigation. Even if we don't think their methods are foolproof, they may have a lead that will make all of this work moot." Please, please be true.

"Because Charles had proximity, motive, and means to do it, and no one remembers seeing him right before Darwin was killed, they are fairly certain that it's him."

I stared at Lucy. "How did you get that information?" I asked, dumbfounded. I definitely wanted to know her tricks.

She gave a little smile and shrugged, "I may have had dinner with Lucas again."

My eyes widened. "Lucy!" I didn't want her ruining a possible relationship just because we could use information.

She held up her hands, "he wouldn't have said anything if it was truly confidential, he's very professional." she said it with a secret smile that made my heart melt. You go girl.

"I know you want to check everyone out, but I'm telling you, it's always the wife." Madeleine said, arranging a couple of poinsettia plants on a shelf.

Ro huffed a laugh.

"What is your problem?" Madeleine put her hands on her hips.

"I'd never trust the judgment of anyone whose parents named her after a French cake." Ro placed a resin vase with swirling blue feathering out around the lip onto another shelf.

Madeliene's eyes widened and she opened her mouth for a retort when Lucy and I both started talking at once.

"I still need to see if anyone else has alibis."

"How are your in-laws settling in?"

With us talking over each other Madeliene probably hadn't heard what was said but she turned back to what she was doing, throwing glowers over her shoulder at Ro.

"Really," I whispered, "you brought up the in-laws? Dump gasoline on the fire why don't you."

"I was desperate! She and Ro would argue all night, I could tell it was brewing."

I stifled a laugh, she wasn't wrong.

"Ah!" Ro snapped. "Darned stalker, what's wrong with you?"

We all turned toward her in time to see our friendly neighborhood music box ghost standing on the other side of one of the bookshelves.

"He sure is insistent." Lucy commented with a little shiver. She clearly wasn't as used to this guy as I was.

"If you could communicate better that would be helpful." I said.

"Or communicate at all." Ro said snidely, giving him an appraising look. "He refused to respond to my interrogation when he interrupted me being sick."

"As long as he's not aggressive, I don't care." I said tiredly. He was better company than my family at least.

Lucy walked over and placed an antler headband on me, clicking something so that it lit up. She smiled. "That's what we need, it's much more cheery." she proceeded to put one on Madeleine but when she got close to Ro, Ro gave her a stern enough glare that she put it on herself instead.

"At least some of us aren't party poopers." Madeleine said pointedly.

They bickered and I had to smile, even amidst their bickering they would always be there for each other In a time of need, we all would. That was why I had to give back, I had to help that child and her dad. It was starting to no longer become a nuisance that I needed to research a bit, it was starting to become very personal to me.

Since Victor Smith wasn't going to be easy to talk to I opted to go to talk to the city attorney. Both he and his receptionist were always welcoming to me. It might have something to with the fact that whenever I went there I brought either coffee or treats. Today I brought both.

Per usual Attorney Blake sat in a chair diagonal to me instead of behind his desk. Steepling his fingers he asked, "what brings you here today, Cammie?" Something in his eyes, maybe a glimmer of amusement, alerted me that he might have an idea.

"I actually just wanted to talk to you about Darwin."

"Ah." He met my gaze and held, "you saw us arguing."

I nodded. "No one I talked to thinks he was a nice man. At this rate I wouldn't be surprised if his own mother disowned him."

"I know you found the body but that doesn't mean you have a responsibility to talk to people that knew him. It wasn't your fault after all."

"I'm aware. I just..." I let my gaze drift around the room, trying to come up with an explanation that didn't include me stating that I was once again going around the police and trying to figure things out myself. As helpful as he'd always been, I didn't imagine he would take kindly to me nosing into more things that should be taken care of by the professionals.

I decided on a half-truth. "The banker, Charles, has a young daughter and she's hurting and asking questions so I wanted to talk to people and just try and find out anything that could help her come to terms with all of this."

He nodded along with everything I was saying, eyebrows knitted. "It's a tragic thing. I have kids too and the idea of them not having me around to be there for them breaks my heart." He sighed, gaze down, and thought for a moment. "Darwin scammed a lot of people out of a lot of money. I'm honestly surprised he wasn't at least beaten up before now. Not that I condone that." He gave me a look. "He didn't respect women, either. The reason we argued was because he was so rude to my wife. He even stole a promotion from a woman. Not because he was the better worker because he certainly wasn't, but because he was able to somehow cajoled their supervisor into it."

I frowned. "That's terrible. How could he get his supervisor to do that?"

"Likely he had something on his supervisor. Or not, he does have a slick tongue when he wants to. Did, I should say. He was also the type who took credit when he had nothing to do with the positive result."

"Nice guy." I muttered. It was beginning to look like Darwin had more enemies than I knew what to do with. But if that were true, then it was less and less likely Charles did it.

"Thank you for telling me all this," I readied to stand.

"You don't think Charles did it and you're not going to let this go, are you?" Anthony Blake stared at me with narrowed, shrewd eyes.

"Oh you know me, just making sure all the i's are dotted and t's are crossed so the family can at least know someone tried."

He didn't comment further, just stood and escorted me out. He didn't believe me. That was okay, as long as he didn't do anything to stop me from looking into this.

One thing he mentioned had given me another direction. He mentioned Darwin's place of work. Why I hadn't thought to go there in the first place I wasn't sure, but I was definitely heading there now.

Darwin had worked at a construction company specializing in luxury housing for the wealthy clientele that built summer homes in this county. They had an office over just off of 18th street and I headed that way.

The office was huge and of course looked phenomenal. They had fake aspens decorating part of the room, giving it a woodsy feel even as the scent of pine from the real pine tree they had decorated in gold and white permeated the air. Everything was perfect. It was beautiful, but I preferred homemade touches, this felt sterile.

I walked up to the front desk where a pretty secretary with her hair twisted in an elaborate updo sat. She smiled at me, "hello and welcome to Whispering Lakes' premier luxury construction company, Woodland Construction, what can I do for you?"

I took a deep breath. There wasn't any good reason they wouldn't turn me away. I was certainly not here to buy—or ask them to construct—an expensive house on the lake.

"Hello," I spoke as calmly as I could, trying to pretend I belonged in a place like this. "I wanted to speak with Jack Russell. Is he in?"

"Do you have an appointment?"

I needed a new tactic and quickly. "Actually I—"

A woman came out of one of the offices, interrupting us. She was familiar, with dark hair, glasses and a fit figure.

She saw me and came over "Hi." The woman said. Where did I remember her from?

"Hello, it's nice to see you again." I said, hoping that she would supply her name or that I could get away with never using it.

"You too. Are you here looking for an addition to your house or possibly something new?"

I weighed my options, I didn't have money and I didn't want to lead her on. "Actually, I'm looking for some closure, regarding your coworker?"

Recognition sparked in her eyes. "That's right, I heard that you're friends with Charles and Jenny. The whole thing breaks my heart."

I finally placed her. Kylie. She'd been at the toy drive and had said she'd worked with the murder victim and that he was a real piece of work. I imagined so, especially after Mr. Blake told me that he was a chauvinist as well. Which didn't surprise me given his personality.

I smiled, "it's been a very difficult time and I'm trying to support as best I can. She really needs closure and I wanted to talk to Mr. Russell about Darwin for a few minutes." I held my breath, would she help?

"He stepped out for a meeting with a client at the construction site, but he shouldn't be gone much longer. I'm happy to talk with you until he comes back if you'd like."

"That would be very kind of you." Yes!

She led me back to her office. It was large, with a mahogany desk and beautiful view of the hills and forest out of the floor to ceiling windows.

"This is a stunning office." I said, admiring the metal artwork on the walls, especially the one depicting a mountain rising behind a dark forest.

"Thank you, I just recently got a promotion." She went to a small fridge, the clear glass door showing bottles of tea, water, and soda inside. "What can I get you?"

"Nothing, thank you. I'm just appreciative of your time."

"Of course." she grabbed an iced tea for herself and came over, sitting next to me in one of the two chairs that sat in front of her desk.

"Congratulations on your promotion."

She blew out her breath as if it was a relief, and gave me a big smile, "It's a dream for me, I've worked here for just about eight years. What exactly did you want to talk about?" Her eyes lit with curiosity and she looked at me intently. Another gossip like Mandy? That woman thrived off of juicy tidbits that she wasn't supposed to know. And sharing them of course.

"First of all I'm very sorry for your loss." I tilted my head a little, trying to look sympathetic. "Though if I do remember what you said at the toy drive correctly, he wasn't the best person."

She shifted, lips pursed. "It's wrong to speak ill of the dead. Those of us here at Woodland Construction are devastated by his loss." Not a single word rang true.

I gave her a conspiratorial smile, "I'm not with the newspaper, you don't have to play a part with me. Not a single person that I've talked to said he's a nice guy. But who would kill him?" I left the question hanging there for a moment and when she shifted again, not answering, I feared that she wouldn't respond at all.

She seemed to give it some thought, then leaned toward me and lowered her voice. "People often know him for his scams, getting people to buy into a business that would then go under and he would sell all the equipment for a profit while the investors got nothing."

What a rat.

"But the thing is, his ex-wife has been trying for some time to get alimony from him. He was ordered to pay it in a divorce, but he never would. She was livid when she came here a few weeks ago. She threw an absolute tantrum in the office." She must have noticed my widened eyes. "Ask anyone in here, it was messy. She told him and I quote, 'if you don't give me that money you'll regret it.'"

"Oh wow." I wondered if the police had gotten that tidbit. Of course they did, they had to do some form of investigating.

A man walked through the open door. He wasn't very tall but he was broad shouldered and fit, with distinguished graying hair.

"Hello." he greeted. "I understand you wanted to talk to me?" His eyes held wariness and suddenly I wondered if he should be on the list of suspects. I would need to find out.

"Mr. Russell." I got to my feet and shook his hand, giving him my best disarming smile, which probably would have been more effective if I were twenty years younger.

His stiff shoulders seemed to relax slightly. "Why don't you come into my office so we can talk."

I said goodbye to Kylie and hurried after him as he strode out of the room and across the open lobby area to his own office. Surprisingly it was simpler than Kylie's, nothing decorated the walls and his desk wasn't nearly as superb. Instead, he had a long table that stood one side of the room with plans laid out on it.

"First of all, I wanted to say sorry for your loss." I told him. I had sat down but he stood next to his desk, not making a move to sit. Okay then. "I'm just here gathering some facts so the family can get a little closure at least."

His forehead creased in a frown. "His family? He and Mandy are divorced, and I don't think he has any family around here."

"Not him, the little girl who just had to watch her dad go to jail. I just want to make sure that I talk to people on her behalf and get the real story. Good or bad, she should know when she grows up what all happened." I certainly hoped he believed my spiel. Technically it wasn't *wrong*, even if I did feel guilty for not being wholly truthful.

He rubbed a hand down his face. "I don't know what everyone else is saying, but he was good with the clients. He was the best at getting extras added on. I didn't socialize with him outside of work, so I can't speak to that. He did his job and didn't give me problems."

I processed what he said. It made sense that he would be good at that kind of a job.

"Is there any reason you gave him a promotion instead of anyone else?"

His brow furrowed and he studied me even as the wariness returned to his eyes. "He did his job, he'd earned it."

"How long did he work for you?"

"Three years."

Hmm.

From the wariness in his face to the tense way he held himself, I knew I wouldn't be getting more out of him.

I stood. "I see. thank you for your time." I turned to go, then stopped and turned back. "Do you have any idea who might have hated him enough to kill him?"

He faltered, then his face closed off. "No."

"Have a good day."

I went home and walked into my house to the phone ringing.

It took me a minute to find where I'd left the receiver—under a throw pillow—before I answered.

"Hello?"

"You have to get down here right now." Madeleine's voice was hysterical.

Chapter 11

Worry seized me. "Slow down, breathe."

She groaned dramatically, "oooh. This just keeps going from bad to worse."

I walked over to where I'd dropped my purse and grabbed it. I had a feeling I wouldn't be spending a quiet evening at home.

"Can you tell me what's going on?"

"Jenny just went in and told them that she did it, that she killed him."

I froze, what in the whacky Christmas candy was going on? There was no way they'd believe a kid did that…right?

"Um, are we sure she didn't do it?"

"Cammie!"

"I had to ask!"

"Are you coming to help us rescue a lost little girl or not?" she demanded.

"I'll meet you…at the police station?" all the ghost pepper seeds would break loose if the chief was there and saw us all march in. He hadn't reacted kindly to our involvement in the manor debacle.

"Yes. See you soon. Bye."

"Bye." I hurried to drag on some outerwear and got in my car, turning Buttercup toward the station.

To say it was chaos in the police station would be an understatement. It would have been calmer if Santa had shown up and started giving out winning lottery tickets.

Even Douglas Shaw, the editor of the newspaper, was there with a reporter, camera in hand, snapping pictures and lobbing questions at the officers.

Chief Papasadoris looked like he was having an allergic reaction to it all. His face was red and puffy, his eyes bulged, and he opened and closed his mouth like a caught fish. I almost felt bad for the man. Almost.

I sidled up too where Madeleine stood off to the side, eyes shooting daggers at the chief.

"You called Douglas?"

"Of course I did. If they were going to arrest a child it needed to be documented in the newspaper so the family could sue later." Madeleine said in a matter of fact tone that belied how mad she was.

Lucy's hopeful gaze was on one of the officers standing next to the chief. Lucas. Things couldn't get worse could they? No I shouldn't ask that, it was never a good idea to tempt fate.

Chief Papasadoris with spluttering to answer a question that I hadn't heard. He finally stopped trying to answer and gestured at Lucas. Dutifully, Lucas stepped forward, calm blue gaze on the reporters.

"The investigation is still ongoing. We haven't made any conclusions yet. Of course we're going to let the young girl go, we understand that she is under a great deal of stress and grief which has prompted this declaration. Quite frankly, she doesn't have the strength to have killed him. So to answer your question, we are letting her go now."

Jenny was brought up from the back, pink backpack in hand. She looked haggard, if a child could look haggard. She saw us and ran over to Lucy, leaving a frustrated officer to gaze after her. Chief Papasadoris pinned us with a look, coming over to our side of lobby.

"I should have known you would be here causing trouble." He said it quietly enough that the reporters couldn't hear.

"What was that?" Madeleine said loudly, "you think we're causing trouble by being here to support a child?"

The reporter was holding out a recording device and got closer as she spoke.

The chief gave her a cool look, and said, "we need to release her to whoever has custody. You can't just come waltzing in and take children."

"Lucy and Jenny are related, and she's an adult, so that would be her." Madeleine said quickly.

I blinked, wondering how much time you could get for lying and if the chief would push it and try to make her prove it.

He didn't. He was studying the reporter out of the corner of his eye and put on what he might have considered a smile. I thought it looked more like a grimace. "Then we'll release the child back to her—" he raised his eyebrows, waiting.

"Umm." Lucy blinked.

"Cousin once removed." I said with a smile. "I always forget that once removed too." I said in an obvious conspiratory way to her.

The chief pinned me with a flat stair. For all his bluster I wasn't concerned about him hassling us more right now, especially not with a reporter right there. Besides, even he wouldn't keep a little girl in a cell overnight to prove a point. Maybe someone who was seventeen or eighteen, but certainly not a child. I hoped.

I stepped over to Jenny and rubbed her arm gently. Her arms were cold and she was covered in goosebumps.

"Come on, get your coat on. Let's go decorate Lucy's shop for Christmas." I met her gaze over the kid's head, hoping she hadn't done it already. We all needed something else to focus our attention on. Jenny was so tense that her shoulders were reaching for her ears.

Lucy produced a strained smile and nodded.

We all trooped out to the parking lot.

"Meet you all there?" I said at my car.

Madeleine shook her head. "I've been gone too long and the in-laws at the house are starting to wonder where I am all the time. My husband keeps texting me wondering when I'm coming home. If he doesn't like his own family enough to be alone with them without me there to help, they shouldn't have come for Christmas." she grumbled.

"Thank you for all you've done Madeleine." Lucy said. "I would have fallen apart without you."

We said goodbye to Madeleine and got in our cars, Jenny riding with Lucy.

She opened up the shop and flicked on the lights. Multiple boxes and some totes waited against the wall.

"Some of this is new that I bought, and some of this is Christmas stuff I haven't used in my house for ages." she explained. "Jenny why don't you help decorate the tree?" she directed the kid over that way while I opened a large box and pulled out a family of light up deer.

"By the time we're through this place is going to look like a Christmas art exhibit." I said.

Jenny hadn't spoken but she nodded. At least she was listening. She was probably exhausted, both emotionally and physically. A renewed sense of urgency filled my chest. I needed to figure this out. I didn't believe that her father had done this, not after the things I'd heard. A killer needed to be brought to justice and Santa needed to be let loose. Easier said than done.

I started hanging lights in the windows while they got to work on the tree. An hour later a knock sounded at the door. Lucy went and got it and I leaned over to see who it was. Lucas. He looked at Lucy, face open, vulnerable, not at all like the work face he'd had on earlier. He swallowed as he gazed into her eyes and it dawned on me that maybe he thought she blamed him for all this. And that I shouldn't be spying on them.

"Lucas." she said softly, a little smile touching her lips she stepped back and waved him inside. "Come on in come on it's cold out."

He stepped in, his thick jacket rustling as he did.

He caught sight of Jenny and she stared up at him.

"Are you here to arrest me?" her voice was so small if that man tried anything I would tackle him to the ground and sit on him so she could get away. I dearly hoped that would never happen.

"Not at all. In fact," he glanced at Lucy and then his gaze flitted to me. I was not given the same soft look, it was more along the lines of a long-suffering expression that crossed his face. "I'm going to talk to Lucy and Cammie and see what they found. I know they've been looking into this and I want to see if I can help. I can't promise anything about your dad though." he said, setting the expectation.

"Cammie said the same thing." she said, not taking her big brown eyes off him.

"Why don't you go back to decorating the tree and we'll go talk for a second, okay?" Lucy led him and I to a small back room that looked like it would become her office. "You're going to help?" She looked at him with the same open, hopeful gaze as Jenny had.

I pinned him with my stare, trying to look intimidating. I knew I wasn't, but I could at least pretend. He better not disappoint those two.

"What do you have so far?" he asked.

"Um, no, you first." It was out of my mouth before I could think better of it. "As far as we understand it, the police think that child's dad did it and they're not looking at anyone else. How can we trust you?"

We faced off and I realized what a foolish idea was to confront a police officer. Too late, I had already dug my grave. Chief Papasadoris would be downright gleeful if I had to spend the night in a cell.

"Listen." Lucy said tiredly. "We're all exhausted, it's late and dark, Jenny is going to come to stay with me tonight and I already called and let her grandma know." she made a face. "Even though she didn't realize she'd been gone in the first place."

Lucas nodded and stepped back, "how about we all meet and discuss this tomorrow?"

She looked at me, "will you do that?" Her gaze implored me and I relented.

"Okay." I met his beautiful blue gaze. "I hope you're being sincere."

"I am." he said firmly.

If we could have him on our side it would be very, very helpful.

Chapter 12

My work, the cultural Art Center, was my haven. It hosted historic books, archives, and displays that depicted the culture and accomplishments of earlier eras. Usually my desk had at least a stack of three books, a map with various international historical moments and where they happened, and a stack of papers for grants that I kept promising myself to get to. I would after Christmas. Or at least that's what I told myself. Today though all of that had been moved and I had a huge piece of white poster board taking up my desk and I was attacking it with a marker ferociously.

The bell dinged downstairs, letting me know that someone had come in. I went around my desk and started down the stairs.

"It's just me." Madeleine's voice came to me. She walked into the giant display room a moment later and I paused on the steps.

I took one look at her and waved her toward my office. "Come up and let me make you some tea. Or would you rather have hot cocoa?"

"Tea is good." she said tiredly.

She made her way up the stairs and into the office, settling into a chair while I turned my electric kettle on to boil. It was fast and a moment later I had tea steeping for her.

"What's wrong?" I sat in the chair next to her.

She rubbed her eyes, smearing her mascara. This was not like her at all. She was a dramatic person, but she was always a polished and classy dramatic person. I reached over and took her hand, trying to give her silent strength.

"I feel like you're the only one who could understand. I don't mean to bring up bad memories though." She started, more laid back than I'd seen her in a long time.

"Don't worry about me, just tell me what's going on." I could already guess the topic of conversation and my family issues were long term and I was used to them.

"I don't know what's wrong, but my in-laws are grating on my nerves more than they've ever had before. Lawrence and I have been married for nearly a decade and a half now and they seem worse than usual." she shook her head, eyes distant. "His parents want us to move into the same neighborhood as them and take care of them." She looked at me with a weary gaze. "Am I a terrible person for being upset with them about that?"

I frowned, surely there must be more to it. "Did you ever promise them that you would, or did Lawrence ever make any kind of indication that he would do that for them so as to make them think that way?"

She shook her head firmly. "We talked about that shortly after we got married and then again a few years back. When my parents were sick we made the decision that we wouldn't move, but we would make sure they had either in-home care or were in a facility, and we would go visit once a month since they were so far away. I know I shouldn't resent his parents, but I really do right now. We're not spring chickens and we're set in our ways and yet they want us to pack everything up and move our entire lives two states over to take care of them? They didn't even suggest coming here."

Her eyes were watery. She was really torn up over this.

"Madeleine, expectations aside, you have to do what you can live with. If you wouldn't forgive yourself for not taking care of them, then you need to think of that and find a middle ground with them. But you can't let yourself be bullied into changing your entire life, either. It must be scary getting older, so maybe they just need some reassurance that even as they get into their nineties, they won't be forgotten."

"They are really dogmatic people." She sighed. "Middle ground isn't a thing for them."

"Then you and your husband maybe should have a private heart to heart." Now I was being a counselor with no relationship experience or qualifications. Great. "I don't know anything about relationships, you know that, but it seems to me that you both would feel better if you stood in unity in this. Maybe talk to him outside the house and away from his parents?"

"That's actually a very good idea. I'll call him and see if he'll meet me for lunch." She let out a frustrated breath. "Not inviting his parents might be easier said than done because they like to guilt trip, but I'll at least give it a go."

She seemed to collect herself and turned her attention back to me. "I'm sorry I haven't been as much of a help to you and Lucy in trying to research who could have committed the murder as I usually could be."

"Don't be." I shook my head. "This isn't our job, and we're entitled to have issues that come up that are a bigger priority."

"Well, I will find a way to make it up to you all." She straightened, sitting taller in her chair.

"All of us? Including Ro?" An impish grin flashed on my face before I could contain it.

She narrowed her eyes at me but the corners of her lips turned up. "Don't push it." she said, humor lacing the words.

We both stood and she gave me an uncharacteristically sappy hug. Before she turned to go she looked at my desk. She glanced back at me before looking at it again and getting closer. "You know this makes you look like a crazy person, right?"

I put my hands on my hips, "I don't know what you mean, it's a timeline and everyone linked to the victim."

"That right there looks like a conspiracy theorist's board. All you need are strings attaching newspaper articles and pictures from one side of the room to the other."

I leaned my head back and groaned. "No one appreciates all my hard work. This is why I live with cats."

After she left I went back to my highly organized, well thought out, non-conspiracy-theorist-looking board to determine what to do next.

I needed to talk to Victor, to find out why he bashed in the man's car. I dreaded it. I'd never seen that man not grumpy a day in his life. Plus, I'd recently been on the receiving end of his yelling. But the only others without alibis were Darwin's ex-wife and of course Charles. Given that his ex-wife was trying to get money from him, she made a very good suspect. A passionate, spur of the moment killing fit an ex-wife perfectly. Especially one having to put up with his nonsense even after the divorce. I'd already talked to her though, so my next to-do was talk to Victor. I needed to find a way get to him though, and then a way to get him to answer my questions without biting my head off. I drummed my fingers on the table.

Going to my phone I dialed Ro. She was working at the library today. Her coworker answered and I asked for her.

"I'll get her. Just be careful, she's in a bad mood." The young woman whispered into the phone.

I almost laughed, she must be new, that was Ro's usual demeanor.

Ro came on the line.

"What?"

"It's always wonderful to hear your voice too Ro." I said.

"I thought it was someone else, sorry."

"It's okay, I'm used to it by now." I chuckled. She did not. "I want to run some of the information I have about the murder by you, if you have a minute."

"Sure." From the tone of her voice she had perked up on hearing that.

After going through everything, a piece at a time, I sighed. "I just don't know what to do first or even how to get more information on Mandy. Or if Victor will deign to even acknowledge my existence let alone talk to me."

"Hmm." She was quiet for a long moment. "You know, Mandy's best friend is Katie, she manages the Luxe Locks hair salon. And as indicative of hairdressers, she's very talkative. I'll see if I can get her to tell me anything that might be helpful."

I closed my eyes and blew out a slow breath. "Thank you so much for your help."

We said bye and hung up. Now the next step left for me was to talk to Victor. I had noticed even the usually courageous Ro didn't want to talk to Victor. I was doomed.

After work I headed to the store. Even though Susie had left half a bag of cat food I'd been feeding Holly Rutherford's higher quality moist food and had run out this morning.

Inside I puttered around the aisles, eventually ending up with everything I needed to make more fudge and cookies in my cart, along with a ham, a bag of potatoes and a bag of mixed vegetables. It was amazing how items just jumped into my cart when all I needed was cat food.

I turned down another aisle and stopped, backing up quickly. My cart squeaked loudly in protest of moving backwards and I winced. Victor Tjernagel was slowly moving down the produce aisle. Part of me, a big part, wanted to turn around and get out of his vicinity. But this was an opportunity I couldn't pass up.

I left my cart and tried to get closer to him without being conspicuous.

Stalking someone through the produce aisle at the grocery store. My mother would be so proud.

As I considered how I could approach Victor and broach the topic of his destroying Darwin's car with his shovel, I caught sight of a familiar face a few feet behind him. What was the ghost doing here? He was staring at Victor and though his face didn't emote there was something in his eyes that made me sad. Were they relatives? Was a ghost even someone who died or was it a different entity? Not expecting any answers anytime soon I compelled myself forward. Victor had something to do with both of my questions and I needed to at least talk to him a little bit. I sure hoped he wasn't as unhinged as his active shovel made him seem.

He glanced up and scowled at me when I walked up to him. I gave him my best smile, trying to convince myself that this was fine and everything was going to be okay and I was not going to get chased down and beaten with that zucchini he held in his hands.

I wasn't sure what to do with him, go in subtle or be blunt. Without fully thinking it through I blurted out, "why are you so angry all the time?"

His bushy eyebrows shot up then lowered, frowning. "I'm not angry." he grumbled.

"Well, you certainly don't seem like a fluffy kitten." My gaze softened as I looked at him, taking in the deep wrinkles, his haunted eyes and downturned mouth. "I'm sorry it's such a hard time of year for you. Trauma during the holidays makes them a painful reminder forever."

He flinched, sightlessly gazing down at the zucchini in his hands. I figured he'd lost someone, maybe his wife.

"I lost everything I loved." He whispered.

Hesitantly I reached out and placed a hand on his arm. He jerked a little as if he wasn't used to human touch. "You're a strong man."

"Not hardly." He scoffed and shook his head slowly, gaze still unfocused. "I wasn't strong enough to keep those I loved."

"That's not your fault." I said softly. Unless he was a murderer. Then it definitely was his fault and I needed to move away, fast. But for whatever reason I didn't think that was the case. That and the rumor mill would have already deposited that information in my lap at some point in my many years here.

"Have you always lived here?"

"Over fifty years." he said.

He seemed so docile now, but I had to keep in mind that under that calm there was someone who had bashed in Darwin's car.

"Victor, I know you're hurting, is that why you attacked Darwin's car?"

He let out a humorless bark of laughter. "Because taking the shovel to him would have been wrong. I wanted to though. Waste of air." he looked at me sternly. "I'm not sad he's gone. I don't believe in that nonsense about not speaking ill of the dead."

I nodded. "I agree. But it sure looks bad that you smashed his car up before he died."

He scoffed, not concerned or affected. "That was weeks ago. He conned everybody he met. I finally was done with him acting like an arrogant swine to everyone around him. He was a gutter rat and yet he treated everyone as beneath him." He didn't get angry as he spoke, just stated them like they were facts. Clearly, to him they were.

"Some people think you killed them." I said carefully.

"Mangey gossips." he finally looked at me, meeting my gaze. "Don't pay them no mind miss Cammie, they talk about everyone."

That much was true.

"Who do you think did it?" I tilted my head, eager to hear his response. I still wasn't sure he hadn't done it.

"Someone who finally snapped under his constant pressure. It was no less than he deserved."

Was there no one in town who liked the man? I didn't mind my family disliking me because I spoke the truth but if everyone disliked me I would wonder what was wrong with me.

"Did you see what happened at the parade?" I asked carefully.

He gave me a knowing look. "I was only there at the end. Before that I was at the urgent care because I'm old and apparently need antibiotics for everything. Dr. Smith at the urgent care on Cutler Avenue. Ask him. And if you think there still was enough time for me to kill him then look at me and tell me you think I could catch a young man."

His body was wracked with old age, causing him to bend a little, and whenever I saw him he was moving slowly.

"Thank you. For being so candid." I smiled.

He looked surprised, peering into my face as if I were pulling one over on him. Finally, he seemed to sense that I was being genuine.

"You're welcome."

I helped Victor get the rest of his shopping done and out to his vehicle. He protested a few times, fussing about clingy women, but I felt bad that he had no one and could at least do this in exchange for all of my "meddling" as he called it.

Worried about him being alone all the time, especially during the holiday, I invited him to come to the cultural arts center when I was there if he needed company. I was not expecting to be called a brazen hussy for the invitation but the glint of humor in his face when he said it kept me from shaking my fist at him.

I saw the ghost one more time before heading back inside to buy the cat food and all the things I didn't need. When I looked again, he was gone. I didn't have the music box in my possession, why had he followed me? I wasn't afraid of him and I'd quickly gotten used to seeing him appear in the oddest places. I had the gut feeling that he simply wanted something fixed and couldn't do it himself. Or maybe I just had indigestion, who knew.

Checking out was a quick process and I loaded my bags into my car.

At home I tried to get through the living room without winding up at the urgent care myself.

"That's not the way to find out if his alibi holds." I informed the cats that were twining around my legs, competing for attention.

"Rutherford, this is beneath you. You don't care about me this much, stop letting Holly influence you."

I made it to the kitchen and gave them their food. The way they ate would make a person think that I starved them, but looking at the extra padding they had proved I wasn't a horrible person who made them go without for days on end like they were acting.

I changed into loungewear and brought the music box into the living room with me. There was something I was missing. Some clue that could help me find the owner and put the ghost at ease.

I washed my hands thoroughly and dried them, then sat on the couch and ran the pads of my fingers around the box again, feeling every little ridge of design and smooth edge. My nail snagged on something, and fear welled in me. Did I just do something to make the precious music box splinter? I lifted it so I could see the bottom and brought it closer to my face. No splinter, but there was the smallest groove with a minuscule knob inside. I pressed the knob with my pinky and nearly dropped the box when a drawer popped out. Heart racing, I stared for a moment before setting it down on the coffee table and delicately pulled out the contents of the drawer. A pink bow hair clip, a lock of blond hair with a ribbon, and a yellowed piece of paper. I unfolded the paper.

To Ariadne, you hold my heart in your precious hands. Love, Dad.

I barely jumped this time when the ghost showed up. I looked up at him, standing a few feet away, giving me space but still hovering close. "Was this yours? Did you make this music box for your daughter?"

He gazed at me solemnly, then purposefully directed his gaze back at the paper. Did he want me to find Ariadne? My shoulders relaxed. I finally knew what to do. He wanted me to deliver this to his daughter. Now all I had to do was find her. I mean, there should only be several thousand Ariadne's in the US, so it should only take me a year to whittle down the options.

"It would be useful if I had a last name." I looked back up to find him gone. "If you're going to keep popping into my life unannounced you could at least be more helpful."

Chapter 13

Christmas was closing in fast and we still hadn't made nearly enough headway to help Jenny's dad.

We all sat around a table at the café, snacking on mini cranberry, orange and chocolate pavlovas and eggnog pudding. It was surreal, to think that someone's life was being thrown into total chaos while we sat here with Burl Ives and Ella Fitzgerald crooning Christmas classics through the speakers overhead.

"What are you thinking about?" Lucy leaned toward me, jolting me out of my reverie.

I tapped a finger on the table, not realizing I'd been so lost in thought. If I told her how I was feeling it would just make her feel down, so I brought up something else I'd been mulling over.

"Something Victor said. Who around Darwin was being constantly pushed around and bullied by him? Not just a one time thing like a scam, but constantly?"

"Besides his wife and his girlfriend?" Madeleine gave me a look. "People closest to us can definitely make us homicidal."

I got the feeling she wasn't referring to the victim anymore.

"The girlfriend has an alibi and when Ro arrives she might have more info on the wife." I hoped.

MILK, COOKIES, AND MURDER

"I feel like there's something missing here, but I just can't put my finger on it." Lucy blew out a frustrated breath. "It's as if there's something on the periphery of all this but I just can't place it."

"Same for me." She understood how I felt and I warmed at the reminder that I wasn't alone in this.

"I hope Ro hurries, I need to get home soon to coddle the relatives." Madeleine grumbled.

My heart hurt for her. She was a giving, caring person, despite her penchant for drama, so if they were driving her to feel like this it was because she had hit the end of her very long, proverbial rope. The idea of being stuck in the same house for weeks with my own family made me feel claustrophobic.

I handed Madeleine a pavlova she took and bit into It.

"Christmas time is the best. You're not judged for eating yummy things. I wish that could be for the whole year." I said, dipping into the little ramekin of eggnog pudding sitting in front of me.

"Hear, hear." Madeleine agreed.

Ro came in a few minutes later, walking straight to the table without ordering anything.

"Oh good, do you have information?" Madeleine said without preamble.

"Madeleine!" Lucy fussed. She turned to Ro. "How are you, how was the doctor appointment?"

"I'm dying." Ro said unceremoniously.

"Um," Lucy opened and closed her mouth, not certain what to say to that.

"I hate to break it to you, but we're all dying." I said, immediately catching on to Ro's dry humor.

Lucy glowered. "That wasn't nice, I thought something was wrong."

"I'm sorry." Ro said, clearly not sorry at all.

I offered her a pavlova but she shook her head. "I don't think it can take any more sugar this month."

"See," Madeleine sent me a disgusted look, "I keep telling you she's not normal."

I didn't want to add fuel to the fire so I changed the subject. "Were you able to talk to Mandy's friend?"

She nodded. "I found out something very interesting, but her excuse for not being at the parade is sketchy. Her friend met her earlier that day and she was just fine."

"That doesn't really prove anything, she could have felt sick later." Madeleine said.

"What's the interesting part?" I leaned forward eagerly.

"Guess who Mandy is seeing on the sly? Any guesses? No? Jack Russell, Darwin's boss." She went silent, watching us absorb that information.

"Well this just got a whole lot more interesting." I murmured. Another motive had popped up.

"That's not a good thing." Madeline said.

"They could have planned the murder together for all we know." Lucy said, eyes wide.

"That's true." I sighed. "I guess I need to talk to him again. I don't think he'll be as receptive a second time." Not that he had been the first time, either.

"It could be that he killed the guy for Mandy and she has nothing to do with it." Ro added.

I would need to see if he had an alibi now. Excitement bloomed, at least I had another direction to head in. Maybe this one would help me shake out something useful. Usually it was good to know who the victim's enemies were, but in this case it was pretty much anyone who had ever been in contact with him which was not helpful. At least so far no one had called me a nosy old bag. That was a plus.

"Now that that's out in the open. You're not really dying, right Ro?" Lucy was still concerned.

Ro sighed. "I have an issue that's genetic, but it's not debilitating."

"Speaking of genetic," Madeleine peered at her speculatively.

That couldn't be good.

"Did you have to change your name and hide when you got out of the CIA?"

Ro gave her an unamused look but surprisingly answered. "No."

"Then, you really don't have any family?"

"I never said that."

When she didn't continue Madeleine pressed further. "Why don't you see them for the holidays, then?"

"What's the game plan?" Ro turned to me.

"I have an idea about where I can, 'run into,'" I made air quotes with my fingers, "Mr. Russell again. I don't know that he'll be willing to talk with me, though."

"You could just be direct and tell him that you know about his affair with Mandy." Lucy suggested.

"But is it really an affair?" Madeleine's eyes widened, "do you think they were seeing each other before she divorced Darwin?"

I thought about it, the pieces clicking into place. "If he knew of her infidelity, it could be the blackmail he needed in order to get his boss to give him a promotion when the other people in the office have been there longer and are more decent people in general."

"That's a thought." Ro agreed. She seemed more docile since Madeleine's invasive questions.

There were just things that we would never know about Ro. Like why, exactly, she'd needed to learn how to pick locks. I wasn't complaining, that particular talent had come in handy a few times, but it was just one of many things we wouldn't ever get to be privy to. It was kind of sad, but I was also happy that we got this version of Ro, the cranky librarian who had a lot of down to earth answers and excellent investigative skills.

"Be careful and talk to him with a lot of people around. If he's the killer then you could find yourself in real danger." Lucy said. "And call the police if you even think you're not safe."

Chief Papasadoris would love that.

That angle would explain why Darwin had been running scared from someone. Jack Russell would make an intimidating figure if he was angry.

"I will."

"I mean it." She warned.

Usually I got fussed at by the other two, now her. I met her gaze, she was very concerned.

"I'll be okay and will make sure to take precautions." I promised.

I wasn't a stalker, but— and I'm well aware there should be no but to that statement—bothering people at work and running into them in grocery stores wasn't the best way to go about chatting with them while their guard was down. So I just happened to find out where and when the December council meeting was being held. One of the topics was construction, and I had no doubt that the man benefiting from all of the easy zoning laws would be there to make his voice heard.

Now I sat in one of the hard, plain wood chairs, wasting my evening in the drudgery that was the city council meetings. I could only hope that Mr. Russell like these more than I did and wasn't in a bad mood after this. I sat there waiting as people filed in to watch the process or to speak to the council on the agreed upon topics, but Jack Russell never showed. I bit the inside of my cheek. I hadn't counted on that. Maybe he would show up at the last minute.

Before long the proceedings started and I shifted uncomfortably. He wasn't coming.

I barely heard what they were saying but a name caught my attention, pulling my gaze away from where I stared at the door.

"Kylie Treadwell representing Woodland Construction." The woman who'd helped me before stood and stepped up to the podium to speak. She wore a trim wool suit and she rocked it.

I was disappointed that Russell hadn't come, but I could talk to her again. Maybe it would be easier too, already having established a rapport with her.

There was a reason that I didn't come to council meetings. The droning on, they're not getting anything done, and the false pacifying were egregious to watch. Finally, when I considered taking a nap to get through the monotony of it, a break was announced. Thank goodness.

I headed to intercept Kylie at a table with water and lemonade dispensers.

"Oh hi. I didn't know you'd be here." I kept my tone even. It was the truth, I didn't know she'd be there.

"Hi, yes my boss has started to hand off some of these representative activities to me now that I have the experience." she said.

"The role seems to fit you, your power suit is fantastic. You walked up there and owned it." I wasn't attempting to flatter her, I really did admire the confident way she had held herself and spoken.

She beamed. "Thank you. It's so nice to hear that."

We stepped away from the table so other people could access the drinks that they wanted and now she fiddled with her cup before leaning in a little. "Honestly, it has been such a long, hard journey to get here. This promotion has been in the works for a long time." She sighed, giving me a look, "women have to work twice as hard if not more, right."

She wasn't saying that as a question so I kept my thoughts to myself, giving her a supportive nod. If she felt that way then good for her for overcoming such a challenge.

"And having to work with someone like Darwin," I shuddered, it wasn't fake, after all I heard about him I fully realized he must have been a terror to work with. "You must have incredible patience."

"Ugh." Her lip curled derisively. "There were days when I thought about quitting, that's for sure."

"It must have been shocking, you being at the parade with your boss when that whole thing happened. Did you see him collapse?"

She blinked, a confused expression on her face. "I was there with my sister, actually. I saw Jack briefly at the beginning, but I think he left quite early. I was nowhere near that area when his death occurred."

"I'm sorry, for whatever reason I thought your boss had gone with you. I didn't imagine him going alone."

"I think that's why he didn't stay long."

Now wasn't that interesting.

"I have to wonder, Darwin was such an awful man, was his wife like him?" Tell me she came to the office, tell me she talked to your boss, give me the details that could help this case.

"Oh my gosh no." she shook her head firmly. "That poor woman. Falling victim to him like everyone else."

"So she didn't come around much, besides that time she threw a fit in the lobby because he wouldn't pay her the alimony he owed her?"

She grimaced, "every time I think of that it just makes me so upset for her. She came around a few times after that. She always talked to the boss so I assume that she was trying to get him to take some of Darwin's pay and put it towards the alimony without his choice. But that's not legal without the court being involved so I'm sure he gently turned her down."

"Jack seems like a stand up guy." I took a sip of my water, casually looking around, trying to pretend that I wasn't absurdly excited about all of this information I was getting.

"He is." She met my gaze, concern on her face. "I hope you don't think I'm being harsh, I really shouldn't be speaking ill of the dead. Please don't think anything of it. It was awful what happened, especially him being killed in that way, what a way to go." She shivered.

I blinked, "oh yeah, it's a harsh weapon to use. What was that called again?"

"An ice pick."

"Right."

How did I miss that an ice pick was the murder weapon? That was important information. Or it could be, at least. It hadn't been in the area where he'd collapsed.

We chatted a bit more, the conversation organically moving to Christmas and family, of which she didn't see often. They lived in another state apparently and she worked constantly, rarely taking time off.

After the break was over I pretended to go to my seat and as soon as she sat down in one of the upper rows, I got up and hurried out. No way did I want to stay for the rest of the evening listening to all that. History was a fantastic thing, but people that had lived through that history usually didn't do a good job of moving things forward and that council needed fresh blood. History was a good reminder of what not to do, and provided knowledge on how to move forward, but generally the younger generation was the one that spearheaded moving forward. What was that that I heard in business class? That the businessman who says "we've always done it this way" has already lost. Something like that. It embodied some of what was wrong with the city council.

I had taken the poster board at home after work and now I scribbled next to Mandy and Jack's names. It was beginning to look more and more like Mandy or her lover had done away with the man. They both had proximity, no alibi, and both had a reason to kill him in a fit of passion. I needed to find a way to see if either of them were having financial trouble. It would explain the escalation into getting rid of him. That sounded like a job for a CIA agent turned librarian. I glanced at the clock. It was too late to call Ro now I would get to her tomorrow. Finally, we were getting some traction.

Chapter 14

"You must think I'm a miracle worker." Ro grumbled over the phone.

"As close as we've got to one." I said cheerily.

"You owe me."

"Can't you put it on the tab of helping a little girl get her dad back?" I knew she didn't really mean it, but applying a little guilt never hurt anything.

"So we're all really convinced he didn't do it." It was a statement, not a question, but I felt compelled to answer it nonetheless.

"Out of pretty much everyone that I've spoken with, Charles doesn't even come close to being as personally affected as some others. It's horrible that he lost his money, but that was over a year ago."

"Alright, I'll see what I can find out about financials."

"Thank you!"

"He's getting out on bail, right?"

"As far as I know. I thought it was today." I said. It was a little relief, but the threat of prison still hung over his and his daughter's head. We would do something about that. We had to.

We said goodbye and hung up.

It had been a long couple of weeks since the parade and I was exhausted. I'm sure it had nothing to do with the ache I had for my family as well. They were good people, I just wish they saw past their own self-interest.

I tucked into a bag of reindeer chow, essentially very sugary chex mix with chocolate, and watched White Christmas, the quintessential classic Christmas movie. Rutherford sat on the other side of the couch and Holly curled up in my lap, purring loudly. It appeared that Rutherford had foregone trying to compete with her. Being affectionate took a toll on his princely emotions apparently.

My phone rang and I snapped it up. "Hello?"

"When are we going to decorate your tree?"

I smiled at the voice. "I know you've been busy so I didn't want to put any pressure on you. I figured you'd come when you had the chance."

"That doesn't work, my darling cousin. I won't come when I have the chance, I'll make time. It's you." Gavin said as if that explained everything.

At least one person loved me for who I was.

"If you want, you could come this weekend, or you could come the day before Christmas Eve or on Christmas Eve." Something occurred to me. "Who are you going to have Christmas with this year?" I shouldn't have assumed.

He paused. "You."

"Gavin?" I extended the syllables of his name as I asked.

"Well your mom is going to try to continue to get you to come have Christmas here with her and my family told me that I was hurting them by not wanting to be there with them. My sister burst into tears of course, inciting it all."

I winced. "Just remember that she's pregnant and she's got a ton of hormones raging through her body." Really, there wasn't that much difference between her before and her now, except for the fact that she was milking the pregnancy attention like nothing else.

"Right." he did not sound convinced at all. "Anyway, I was thinking you probably would want to spend it with your mom." He left the door open for me to decide.

"I really would rather have a peaceful Christmas. And I'd love if you came. But don't feel pressured if you'd rather be somewhere else, I have my cats."

He groaned. "Don't ever say that to your mom, she already thinks that you're an old cat lady because you won't date." His voice turned humorous. "You know, I could set you up to bring a date to the next family event, after Christmas. I'll bet they'd never pressure you to date again." he snickered.

All I could envision was a fifty year old biker with long gray hair pulling into a ponytail wearing a bandana, leather pants, and a vest. It was tempting, but then again I could never live it down. Ever. I would hear my mom complain about my lack of taste for ages to come.

Still, there was a petty part of me that like the idea. "I'll think about it."

We decided that he would come tomorrow, Saturday. It was an excuse for both of us to stay out of the weekend luncheons we were invited to.

After we said goodbye I turned the TV back on but my attention wandered. I had done some research, even going so far as to pay a website service that could help me look up people, but there were too many Ariadnes and not enough background information. For all I knew she could have passed away by now. If only I had a date of birth or even a last name. Last name.

Like a hit in the gut, a realization came to me. I had an idea. It was a crazy one, but then again when were normal ideas every helpful. I hurried over to the box and my laptop hoping I was right, and searched for information about a new person.

Saturday came and I had plates of bacon, pancakes, scrambled eggs, rolls, and fruit set out for Gavin's arrival. It was the same breakfast I had made him on the days he had exams when he had lived with me because I was closest to his campus and his parents disapproved of his choice in most everything. It was easier to live with me because I didn't care what choices he made, as long as he was safe. Eventually he realized that he didn't want to get an expensive degree that wouldn't earn him much and put him in an office position where he couldn't be creative. One evening we sat down together and went through all the technical and creative options. He'd always been tactile and charismatic, so he gravitated toward hair styling and now he was a well known colorist who taught at conventions and owned his own salon.

I left the door unlocked for him and he came in while I was in my bedroom, pulling out extra warm, fluffy blankets for him.

I made my way back into the living room.

"Cammie, you have an invader." he informed me from where he was crouched on the floor giving Holly attention while Rutherford looked on In disgust. "It's a sweet, furry invader."

"Be careful, I might think you mean that the mouse came back." I said with a grin, referencing when he and my mother had stayed and a mouse had gotten into the house. Oh the havoc *that* had caused. I hadn't had a problem with mice since but would give him the heebie jeebies nonetheless, to my amusement.

He popped to his feet, his face serious. "Don't test me Cammie, I will get back up on your table again before you can say 'uncle'." he warned, but his eyes were crinkled with humor.

He caught sight of the table with all the plates set out and his eyes were rounded. "I am in heaven." he announced. "What can I do to help you so we can dig into this delicious breakfast?"

I glanced at the clock. It was nearing one pm but knowing him he'd probably rolled out of bed not that long ago.

"There's nothing left to do, just dig in and enjoy it."

We settle down at the table and he snuck the cats a bite of this and that.

"You're going to make them fatter." I smiled.

"It's Christmas. Santa, a fat old man, is the representative of the season, of course we're all going to get fat this time of year." said my skinny cousin, who would never been anything but skinny. When he was a teenager I was worried he would blow away, he'd filled out since then but he was still lean.

"Is there a theme or any ornaments in particular you want?" I had brought a few boxes out, but I had more in my storage closet should I need to pull them out.

He hummed. "Do you remember when you and I and our moms went to that ornament making class?"

"The one with the ceramics?" That was years ago.

"That one. I'd like to add those to the tree."

"Good call." I loved those. They were filled with happy memories and laughter as we tried to outdo each other and had made disastrous messes. Of the three ornaments we had each done, only one turned out well for each of us, the others a reminder of how much fun we'd had slapping on paint and being creative before they were fired and glossed.

"Also, I know how much you love blown glass so I got this to put on the tree." he pulled out an object wrapped in bubble wrap and handed it to me.

I carefully pulled the tape off and rolled it out, revealing a beautiful, glass blown teardrop shaped ornament. It had rich purple swirls around inside it, fading and darkening with each swirl. It was enchanting.

"This is beautiful!" I give him a hug. "Thank you."

"Yes, well," he tilted his head to the side, "you make the best fudge so I have to stay on your good side." Despite his dismissal his bright eyes betrayed his happiness.

Besides ornaments that our grandparents had passed down, along with the ones we've made in our younger years, we pulled out red berry garland to sweep around the tree, pine cones sprayed a brilliant gold we're tucked into the branches in clusters, and red and gold ornaments in varying shapes and designs. The Christmas Song by Nat King Cole soothed my mind as we worked around the tree and we decorated in companionable silence, occasionally reminiscing as we pulled out ornaments we'd forgotten about.

"This one was the result of Grandpa Glen trying to give grandma something that was handmade because that's what she liked the best." I held it up.

Gavin stared. "It looks like the cross between a demon and Santa. Wait, isn't that Krampus?"

I burst out laughing, "Gavin!"

"What? It's true!"

"At least he tried."

"I can't believe grandma didn't go running away screaming."

I continued chuckling, even as I tucked it back into the box. Gavin arched an eyebrow at me, "what, you don't think it deserves a place of honor on the tree? Tsk, tsk."

I ignored him, reaching for another ornament to unwrap. An extended version of Little Jack Frost Get Lost, sung by Seth MacFarlane and Norah Jones, came through the speakers. I swayed my shoulders to the jaunty tune.

Suddenly Gavin grabbed my hand. I looked up in surprise as he pulled me to an area of my living room that didn't have any Christmas clutter.

"What—" I saw his huge, cheeky grin as he held out his hand. We'd gone to jive lessons to support a local dance studio that was new to the neighborhood many years ago when I still lived in Chesterton.

That was when I was young and less brittle. I'm going to break an ankle.

I ignored my internal warning, grabbed his hand, and we danced around in a very loose version of the jive, probably not keeping correct time with the music, and loving every single moment.

We both twirled in opposite directions and I barely avoided falling over the coffee table, laughing so hard I had tears in my eyes.

We both flopped down onto the couch. I was breathing hard and he was still laughing under his breath.

"Do you want to take a break from decorating to watch a movie?" I asked.

He nodded. "I'll make some hot chocolate and grab those snowman shaped eggnog macaroons I brought if you want to find a good Christmas movie to watch.

I chose one I knew he hadn't seen and would be pleasantly surprised by. A few minutes later he brought in a tray with the cookies and hot cocoa and sat down.

His eyes widened, "we're watching an animation?"

"Do you not like animations?" I snagged a macaroon.

"No, they're fine, I'm simply surprised you would like them."

"This one is really good, it's the Grinch, it came out in 2018. And you know how I hate the live versions. But this one's worth watching, very heartwarming."

We tucked into our respective seats and I took a sip of my hot cocoa as the beginning credits rolled. I coughed and sputtered and looked over at my cousin who was wearing a mischievous Cheshire cat grin.

"What did you put in this?"

"Nothing much, just some peppermint schnapps." He said innocently.

I groaned, but it was actually quite good so I needed to be careful, otherwise I would be dancing around the living room without needing accompanying music.

The time went by too fast as it always did, and before I knew it we were at the end of the movie.

"You're right, that was good." He shifted to face me better. "You've been more busy than usual this Christmas, anything you're particularly invested in?"

I thought about telling him about the murder and how I was looking into it, but he didn't need to know the details or that I was neck deep in an investigation I had no real right to be part of. The music box came to mind.

"Actually," I untucked my feet from underneath me and got up with a huff. It was all that Christmas goodness I'd eaten and I wasn't one bit guilty about it. "Can you help me find a person?"

He groaned. "This again. I need to start my own PI agency so you have to pay me." He said it with a joking smile, reaching his hand out for the papers I held.

"This is what I've got so far, but I need to narrow it down for sure." I was so close to the answer, I could feel it. That and the ghost had been hanging around more often.

He looked from the pages to my face, shock widening his eyes. "Cammie, did you actually use the Internet to find all this?" He didn't let me respond, giving me a big smile and spreading his arms wide. "Welcome to the twenty-first century life my history encrusted cousin."

I gave him a little curtsy. "Why thank you, good Sir."

He agreed to do some research of his own, being infinitely more adept at poking through the Internet and social media sites.

We finished up the tree, packing away the rest of the items again before carrying the boxes to my storage closet.

The rest of the day was filled with fun, games, and laughter and I made chicken tetrazzini for dinner.

"Mmm, I'm so feel like a burst." he patted his flat stomach.

"You need to put some meat on those bones."

"You sound like grandma."

I grimaced. "Don't tell my mom."

We clean the kitchen, put everything in the dishwasher and then sat down to watch Scrooge before bed. He planned to leave tomorrow morning but knowing how late he slept I imagined it would be early afternoon.

I pulled the blanket tighter over me and click the fireplace remote so it lit up, casting pleasant dancing shadows around the dim room. This could be what heaven was like.

Chapter 15

Sunday after Gavin left, Ro called.

"I did some digging and it turns out that Jack Russell is in a great place financially. He rakes in the money actually. Mandy doesn't make nearly as much, of course, but she does fine for herself. No debts that I can see, and I have a feeling that the alimony was simply a statement more than a need for her."

"Well then that's a bust. Still doesn't clear them from a passion killing." I mused. "How did you get the info?" She'd gotten it quickly and financial information was hard to get from people.

"You don't want to know."

"Okay then. If you told me you'd have to kill me?" I said, quoting the old cliché.

"Do you know how much work it is to get rid of a body? No way."

"I should feel relieved, but the fact that you know that actually makes me very concerned."

She laughed. "What's the next step? You still need to talk to them and see if they mess up and say anything that could show us that one of them did it."

"Why me?" I demanded.

"Because you get some strange satisfaction out of helping people and I quite frankly have paid my dues and will only do it if it helps one of you."

Ro was honest, and she was a good person even if she was disenchanted with the world after whatever she did in the CIA. I respected her boundaries and appreciated whatever she was willing to help with.

"I don't feel right just going back into his office again and talking to him."

"Do what I did with Mandy's friend. Stalk him and find out where he goes and then bump into him there."

I winced as the image of me hiding behind cars as I followed the man along the sidewalk only to wind up running into the police officer and getting arrested paraded through my mind.

"Can that be plan D?"

She was silent for a moment, then she said, "I'll bet I know where he spends time at after work."

That would be so helpful. "Where?"

"Rudy's Rustic Brews." she said, mentioning the brewery in town. It was fairly famous, selling its beers all over the state and even to neighboring states.

"I can't go there alone!" I protested.

"It's not like it's a business of ill repute, Cammie." I could hear the eye roll in her voice.

I huffed, indignant. "What I'm saying is, it looks weird when only one person goes. Some lonely soul at the bar."

"What you're telling me is, you're not going to take a perfectly good opportunity to determine if someone committed a murder just because you feel uncomfortable sitting by yourself?"

"Yes, that's exactly it."

"Don't you go to movies at the theater by yourself?"

"It's dark and people don't stare there." I defended, knowing it was a losing battle. I would just have to buck up and do it.

"If anyone stares at you stare back until they think you're a psychopath and look away." she suggested unhelpfully.

"I'll add that to the list of things I'm never going to do, but I will go. Hopefully he's there Monday after work. They must have normal work hours, right?"

"He probably gets out a little bit later than the other employees, I'd go there around six-thirty." she said.

"Okay, I will." I paused, "hey, I have a question to ask you."

"Sure thing."

"I have a commitment I have to go to, would you come with me?"

"It depends what it is but I can probably make it."

"Great. See you at Rudy's Rustic Brews at six-thirty on Monday."

She groaned while I grinned.

"I walked right into that didn't I?"

"Yes, yes you did."

"Fine. But I'm not doing the talking if we do see him."

"Great, sounds good!"

"Don't sound so excited, I fully believe in never forgetting or forgiving."

I laughed. "I'll owe you one."

We said goodbye and hung up. I was ridiculously happy knowing I wouldn't be doing this alone, and hopefully we would make some headway. Lately it felt like I was just treading water.

Later in the day a group text popped up, initiated by Madeleine, excluding Ro of course.

Madeleine: *so, how did your date go?*

I waited for Lucy to reply, adding Ro to the chat myself. It always was this way, both Ro and Madeleine excluded the other knowing that either Lucy or I would include the other one. They were odd that way.

Lucy: *it was dreamy! He's such a nice guy!*

Ro: *did he behave himself? Do I need to make him disappear?*

I laughed to myself. That was Ro's way of showing her love, threatening to make people who upset us disappear. I swear after Danny cheated on Lucy she almost said yes to Ro's question, and I had a feeling Danny would have been threatened out of town at the very least.

Lucy: *he was such a gentleman! He gave me a kiss on the CHEEK goodnight when he dropped me off!*

I laughed and added: *it's too early for him to be so forward.*

Lucy sent a laughing face.

Ro: *so will there be a second date?*

Madeleine: *don't worry if he didn't invite you yet, you know its etiquette to wait a few days before contacting the person you went out with to ask for another date.*

Ro: *etiquette is for the birds and people from the 1800s. so will there be a second date?*

I chuckled at their bickering.

Lucy: *I guess we skipped proper etiquette because we're going out again on Thursday.*

I tapped through my phone's overwhelming number of options until I found the little dancing person emoji and sent it.

Madeleine: *I hope this date's more imaginative than just dinner.*

Lucy: *I think so he said that he wanted to take me somewhere but it's a secret.*

Ro: *abort mission. Take you somewhere secret? We don't know that he's not some creepy serial killer!*

Madeleine: *that sounds romantic, good for him.*

Me: *just text when you leave and when you get back.*

Lucy: *it's not for a few days so don't stress. I'll definitely text.*

Madeleine: *and give us more deets on the first date when we see you next.*

Me: *deets?*

Ro: *details. Our oldest member is a teenager at heart.*

Madeleine: *don't be jealous because I'm adaptable.*

Lucy: *okay ttyl, I love you guys!*

TTYL? What was with people and not typing out the actual words? What did they do with the whole half a second they saved not typing it out properly? I didn't want to seem like more of a nincompoop so I googled it instead of asking. *Talk to you later.* Ah, okay.

I got the feeling that I was the least "adaptable" out of all the historical society members, but I was okay with that. There was a reason I lived in a small town that changed very, very slowly.

Monday night rolled around and I dug through my clothes wondering what on earth one should wear to a bar. Something I didn't mind smelling like beer? I eventually opted for simplicity. A pair of jeans, a white turtleneck, in a red crocheted cardigan.

I shouldn't have worried. Walking into the brewery I saw Ro already sitting at the bar. She had faded jeans, winter boots, and hadn't taken her puffer jacket off. She was a much better choice than Madeleine, who would have come likely in heels an address with a long wool coat over it and stood out painfully.

I joined her. "See him yet?" I asked softly.

She dragged her eyes away from whatever sport was being played on the screens in front and above us. "He's right where the bar curves around to the side we can't see. Be subtle when you look."

I leaned back, trying to see around the curve that was blocked by a massive wall of bottles of alcohol. My chair tilted back on two legs and I scrambled to grab onto the counter. Both Ro and the surprisingly fast bartender grabbed on to me.

"Thank you." I said with a shaky smile at the bartender.

Ro grumbled at me, "what part of 'be subtle' did you not understand?"

"Clearly all of it." I glanced back, I could just barely see the side of his head and left arm. "I didn't catch his attention."

"You would make an awful spy."

The thought horrified me. "Oh my goodness I could never. I would give up all state secrets if I was tortured. Or even threatened to never get chocolate again."

That made her chuckle.

She already had a beer in front of her and the bartender asked me what I wanted, being very nice to not mention that I was already clumsy enough that drinking probably wasn't in the best interest of keeping my bones intact. It had to have been years since I last had a beer, opting usually for wine at any events and gatherings with the historical society. Mainly because Madeleine always brought wine, and so did my mother.

"The dark amber is good." Ro recommended after I paused for too long.

"I'll have that then."

"How are we going to start a conversation with him?" I worried.

"Well if you keep glancing over there like you're about to go steal something from him, he's not going to want to talk to us at all."

I sent her a glare. "I most certainly am not, I'm just... assessing the situation."

"Mhhm."

I sipped on my beer, trying to keep myself from looking over too often.

Jack had a companion he'd been talking to but eventually the guy left, while our target ordered another—was that a whiskey? That might be helpful.

"I say we go say hi now."

"I'll be right behind you." Ro said, finishing up her beer while I slipped off the stool.

What if he thought I was a weirdo? Goodness, *I* thought I was a weirdo for doing this. All I wanted was to scurry for the door. But this wasn't about me, that little girl needed closure and her dad needed help if he really didn't do it, which I was beginning to think was fact. Me getting information would hopefully be helpful to that end.

I walked around the bend in the bar and stopped as he looked up. I plastered a smile on my face. "Funny to see you here, Mr. Russell. How are you?" I said as warmly as I possibly could muster while my heart raced in my throat.

"Hi, please call me Jack. Cammie, right?"

"Yep." I took an audacious leap of courage and pulled the tall bar stool next to him out and took a seat.

"Besides the obvious, things have been going quite well. My work always slightly decreases this time of year, but it makes up for how fast and hard will be working this summer." He answered my question.

"Are there a lot of new houses going up?" I asked, truly curious.

He nodded. "People don't seem to realize how big this lake is. We have homes clustered close to town around the lake, but there is a whole half, more than half, of the lake that is vacant and can be built on."

I didn't mention that I hoped the whole lake wouldn't be flooded with luxury homes and that some of the wilderness would stay pristine as it was. Given that he made his money through progress and I liked things to stay the same, we had very different motivations.

I continued to engage him, talking about his work, which he seemed to thoroughly enjoy. Apparently he was a third generation construction worker, and he'd finally decided it was time to open his own business twenty years ago.

"That's impressive." I said earnestly.

Slowly I got the conversation around to Darwin.

"If you ask me, I think they have the wrong man. I think that his ex-wife did it." I said, baiting him. "A lot of people think that actually, she doesn't seem to have an alibi and she definitely has the most motive."

His eyes flashed.

"It wasn't Mandy!" Mr. Russell snapped loudly.

He caught himself and a flustered expression crossed his face even has his ears turned red. He sighed and closed his eyes for a moment before looking back at me. "I'm sorry for yelling. It really wasn't her, you have to believe me." He stared at me with imploring eyes. I wanted to just say "I believe you" and leave it at that, but I couldn't.

I cleared my throat, hating that I had to push forward with this, and wanting to just get up and leave. Ro would have been more suited for this confrontation.

"I truly want to believe you Mr. Russell, but there's no proof. Just because you think she's a decent person doesn't mean she didn't kill him. He was probably an awful husband and then when he wouldn't even give her alimony she probably snapped. I mean, how well do you really know her?" I said it firmly, believing now more than ever that it was her.

He dragged a hand down his face. His expression was one of disbelief, as if he couldn't believe this was happening to him. He let out a humorless laugh. "Even in death he haunts us both." He sighed and seemed to cave. "I know she didn't do it because she was with me. She'd spent the night and we spent the day together at my cabin. I went early to buy some things from a shop but we weren't even in town when he was killed."

I frowned, that didn't add up. "Then why would she lie, and say that she was sick?"

"Because we didn't want him using it against her, going back to court saying that she was cheating on him with me when they were married." He flinched a little, not looking at me. "We did start before they were fully divorced." he met my gaze, his own earnest. "They were already separated by then though."

I shook my head. "Mr. Russell I'm not here to judge. You can't lie about an alibi though." I warned. I understood that he was trying to protect her, but a false alibi would help no one.

"Here." He reached over and grabbed his phone off the bar counter, tapped in a few times and pulled something up onto the screen. "This is my camera from the front of my cabin. Look at the date and timestamp."

I glanced at the date and the time stamp in the top right corner, and then watched as a vehicle drove up and he and Mandy both got out. She was talking, making grand gestures as Mandy often did and he was smiling. It would have been a whole lot easier if this had been shown to me sooner. So if neither of them did it, who was I missing? Regret clutched at me. Clearly I'd missed something important, but I didn't know what or how to find it.

"Thank you for being honest." I said, getting to my feet. I turned to leave and then turned back to him, "I hope you're both happy, you seem like very good people." I wasn't so sure about Mandy, she had her moments, but he certainly seemed like a solid character.

Ro was nowhere in sight when it went back around the bar, so I made my way toward the door, looking back and forth across the room. There she stood, next to the exit.

"You abandoned me."

"No I did not. I just had more faith in you than you did."

Well then, I guess that was that.

We walked out together.

"What did he say?"

I tapped my fingers on my thigh, thinking. "Let's all get together and talk about this. I think we need to reassess."

"Okay." She said slowly.

I dug my cell phone out of my purse as soon as I was standing by my car and made a conference call. One by one the ladies answered.

"We need a new game plan, anyone up for hot cocoa and gingerbread cookies at my house?"

"Sure." Lucy said.

"How about my house?" Madeleine suggested.

Silenced reigned for a moment, then she let out a disgruntled huff. "I promise my in-laws won't eat you, they're more the slow cruel death type. We'll hide out in the sitting room, it has glass doors I can close."

"Only if you have gingerbread cookies." I said.

"If you bring those, I'll furnish the hot cocoa. The best you've ever had. I make it the French way." she said with pride.

"Is that the same recipe book your parents got your name from?" Ro asked into my phone over my shoulder.

I couldn't help it, a chortle escaped before I could contain it and I clamped a hand over my mouth.

Dead silence.

"Have you ever heard that it's a bad idea to anger someone who's making you a beverage?" Despite her probably initial reaction, Madeleine sounded more amused than annoyed, though she'd never admit it. "By the way, not related at all, do you have any severe allergies?"

"Oh my goodness. Ro, stop throwing barbs. Madeleine, please don't poison anyone. We have enough problems as it is." Lucy moaned.

This brought a round of laughter from all of us.

"Okay, your placing in an hour?" I asked.

"See you all then."

An hour and a half later I was tucked into an oversized chair, wrapped in a fluffy blanket with cute polar bears on it and deciding that I never wanted to leave. Madeleine's house was decorated like you would see in a magazine. Luxurious wreaths garlands bows and huge bulbs all decorated different parts of the house. Even the staircase had lights and garland wrapped around each support. Her tree had to stand 7 feet, and it was decorated in a beautiful light silver and rose gold bows and big bulbs. A shining star sat at the top. On the mantle an angel was displayed. It looked like a fairy tale. I half expected the prince from The Nutcracker to walk out from behind the tree. To my disappointment, he didn't.

"Tell us, what's the deal?" Madeleine asked after closing and locking the doors to the sitting room.

Ro muttered something about it being a pretentious name for room. I thought it was delightful.

I got them caught up. "I need your help reassessing every single person in his life. All the people we thought were most likely to do it have been cleared."

Lucy sighed heavily in frustration. "We shouldn't have to be doing this anyway. Lucas said that the chief is difficult to deal with and it's hard to get approval for extra investigations."

Ro raised her eyebrows. "He said that?"

"Not directly. He implied it when I mentioned how little the chief seemed to be doing." she said.

"That doesn't bode well." I muttered. But the truth was that it wasn't something that surprised me. I was just disappointed.

"Okay, show us your murder board."

"My—" my eyes grew big, "oh no, no, no. It's not a murder board like in the movies."

"So what is it?" Lucy asked, the corners of her lips tilted up.

"It's just a posterboard that I've put the names of people who are likely suspects on."

"Don't be a ditz, that's the definition of a murder board. You are now dubbed a sleuth." Madeleine said.

I groaned and placed my face in my hands. "I really don't want labels."

That brought a round of chuckles.

"Okay, let's get down to business on the not-a-murder board." Ro said.

We all gathered around.

"Let's start by grouping everyone from each part of his life. Personal, financial, work, hobbies etc." Madeleine said.

"It'll be easiest to start with his work." I popped the cap off my marker.

"I'll pull up their website and go to the *Meet the Team* tab." Lucy pulled out her phone.

By the time we were done nearly two hours had gone by and Lucy and Ro had looked through his social media to see people he was interacting with.

"Wait, you missed a name." Madeleine pointed at the social media commenter's name.

"I have a feeling his grandma who lives in Florida and thinks everything he does is 'terrific' doesn't need to be on the list of potential suspects." I didn't add her.

There were still people missing, we all knew it. People he dealt with that weren't on his social media, that weren't obvious about their interactions with him.

"It's like we're looking for a specific piece of hay in a haystack." Madeleine dropped back in her chair.

"It's not quite that bad." Ro said. "But we could use some professional help." she turned her gaze to Lucy.

Her eyes rounded. "I do know a counselor, I went to college with her."

"Not that kind of professional help." Rose said dryly.

"Ro, we can't ask Lucy to drag Lucas into this." I stared down at the names, trying to will them into revealing something. They were becoming blurry by this point. I kept being drawn back to the ones that seemed to gravitate around him. But so far we'd hit nothing but alibi dead ends.

"He's a strong man, he can say no if he doesn't want to answer something. I think we should at least try." Lucy said. "Besides, he asked about you all anyway since he always sees me with you."

"I feel like you should let him meet your other friends first. Better to ease him into the crazy." I said.

"Hey!" Madeleine said.

Lucy grinned. "If he can't take you Ladies then he's probably not the guy for me. So how about we all meet to have a dinner celebrating my shop opening soon?"

"I'm game." Ro said

"Yes, but I don't know that you should invite *her* if you want to make a good impression." Madeleine said, sending a glance pointedly at Ro.

I just smiled. I didn't want this to affect her relationship, no matter what she said. I should talk to Lucas on my own.

Chapter 16

Instead of taking me back to his office in the precinct Lucas asked if I wanted to go for a walk. I wondered if it was because there were nosy people about, or if he just liked breathing in ice.

"What can I do for you Cammie?"

I had to be careful with what I said. "As you know, Lucy is invested in Jenny and seeing her doing better because she's been horribly distraught as I'm sure you can imagine. As far as that goes, we have some ideas that might pan out, but we wanted to ask you some questions."

His eyebrows rose as I glanced up at him. "That was very vague."

I sighed. "I know. I just don't want anything that we ask you or talk to you about to affect anything between you and Lucy."

He smiled a brilliant smile and it was if his blue eyes were laughing at me. His smile was like sunshine and it made you want to smile back. "Is this about the dinner?"

I nodded, swallowing.

"I already talked to Lucy. It's not going to be an issue, if there's something that I can't talk about I'll simply tell you. And I really like Lucy, so unless she's the murderer or she does something terrible I intend to continue to try and woo her."

Relief swelled through me and I finally let myself smile. "She's worth it."

He nodded, "I got that."

"Okay then, well I guess I should leave you to your work. Thank you for seeing me."

"Cammie?"

I turned to face him.

"Thank you, for looking out for Lucy and for being honest."

I smiled and left. My relief was palpable. I had felt so guilty that we might affect this budding relationship, but now I felt much lighter and there was hope, hope that maybe we could finally pin down the elusive person who seemed to linger like a shadow on the periphery of where we were looking.

The next day we all met at the restaurant. It was surprisingly barren, with only a few scatterings of people at the tables throughout the carpeted room. Christmas music crooned through the speakers and the scent of peppermint permeated the air. Strange for a pizza place, but still wonderful.

Madeleine arrived there first and had chosen a table in an alcove, giving us some privacy.

I scooted in next to her. Lucy and Ro came around the same time.

Lucy shrugged out of her coat and hung it on the back of her chair. "Lucas might be a little late." she said. "He said to not wait and just order for him."

"Oh my, you're already to the stage where you're ordering his food for him when he's late." Madeleine said, a sparkle in her eyes.

Lucy blushed, a bright pink tinge across her freckled cheeks making her look very much like an elf. She just needed the pointed ears.

"What did he order? What a person eats says something about them." Ro said.

"Does that mean that you're the epitome of a dried up raisin? Because you eat so many healthy raisin muffins? Or a stringy carrot." Madeleine was on a roll. "Or a—"

"He asked me to order him lasagna." Lucy hurried to interrupt the diatribe.

Ro looked like she still was going to send a rebuttal Madeleine's way so I jumped in as well. "Do you have any idea what his plans are for Christmas?"

"His mom lives in Chesterton so he's going to drive up there for Christmas Eve and Christmas Day." she said, a grateful look in her eyes.

Lucas got to the restaurant at the same time as the food was coming out.

"You have impeccable timing." I said in way of greeting.

He chuckled. "I try." He settled into the seat next to Lucy.

When they looked at each other his face softened, and hers brightened. I felt privileged to see one of my dear friends bloom in love. Not that it was love, not yet at least. But they certainly had developed an affection for each other in the short amount of time they'd known each other.

We dug into the food, chatting about light topics.

When the food was nearly gone Lucas finally sat back in his chair. "Let's get started. I know you're doing things behind the scenes, and in order to help you I need all of the details. As you're going about telling me what the deal is, please make sure to be totally honest. That's the only way I can know what you need so I can help you."

We proceeded to spend the next forty-five minutes catching him up, each one of us taking a turn on the things we thought were important for him to know. He sat back and listened without much facial expression. Probably his officer training.

When we were done he blew out a breath and looked at me. "Look at you going all Magnum PI, you even set up a murder board."

"It's not a murder board!" I was appalled.

Ro nearly choked on the water she was drinking.

We discussed it some more and Lucy brought up a good point.

"Would it be safe to rule out all those people that aren't very close to him, even if they've been hurt by him?"

I nodded, "that would make sense, wouldn't it? Killing someone with an ice pick is pretty personal."

Lucas's gaze zeroed in on me, narrowing cooly as he took me in. "Cammie," he said slowly, carefully, in a tone that made me freeze. "We didn't release that information to the public, so how do you know what was used to kill him?"

I blinked, surprised. That was strange. Maybe Kylie was friends with Tammy, the county clerk and recorder and that's how she found out. Tammy had a bead on the pulse of everything in Whispering Lake.

As I mused I realized everyone was staring at me, especially Lucas with a hard gaze. Suddenly my mind went blank before a terrible realization struck me. Ghost pepper seeds. He thought I was the one who killed him!

"What are you suggesting?" Madeleine demanded angrily, turning to him.

I held up my hand to ward off any arguing. Lucy leaned away from him, concern etching her face, and he cast her a regretful glance. Of course, he had to do his job.

Suddenly, it all made sense. The person on the periphery of our investigation was revealed.

"I think I know who the killer is." I blurted, my eyes widening as I realized we'd been chasing in the wrong direction all this time. "I was told about the ice pick by Kylie Treadwell. I assumed she knew because she's friends with Tammy and Tammy knows almost everything of what goes on in this town, including the privileged stuff." It was true but would he believe me? Weren't police supposed to be skeptical? Or I suppose if they weren't they got there very quickly in their line of work.

A moment ticked by as he studied me. I could barely breathe. Did I just set myself up to get arrested? I could hardly prove my innocence inside jail.

He reached for his jacket. No, oh no. He was going to arrest me and take me to jail. I wouldn't do well behind bars and my family would finally take the extra step of disowning me entirely.

"I guess we have high priority murder suspect to investigate." He stood.

What?

"Really?" More than one of us said at the same time.

"We're following a lead. Nothing wrong with that." His face softened when he looked at Lucy as she gazed up at him. She looked at him differently than she had looked at Danny. I knew she had loved Danny, but this was different, even though they had only known each other a very short time it was somehow deeper. It was felt more than seen, the chemistry that flowed between them. I glanced at Madeleine who was studying them. Clearly I wasn't the only one who noticed. She winked at me.

"Well then, let's get this show on the road." Ro said, unceremoniously getting to her feet.

We all stood, pull down our thick winter coats, and made our way toward the door.

I wasn't paying attention, fiddling with my purse, when Lucy stopped suddenly. I nearly crashed into her and pivoted. What the heck—? My eyes widened as my gaze followed hers.

"Danny?" Lucy stood rooted to the floor, shock on her face.

Chapter 17

"Hey, sweetie." He smiled a bashful smile, as if he were shyly introducing himself to a girl he thought was cute. The underhanded cad.

"What are you doing here?" Madeleine barked.

Ro went to stand next to Lucy, narrowing her eyes at him. All the while, my gaze was on Lucas. His keen eyes glanced from Lucy's face to the new guy and anger sparked in their depths.

Danny barely acknowledged Madeleine, having known her for a while since he'd dated Lucy for a couple of years before cruelly cheating on her and breaking her tender heart. He knew that Madeleine blustered, but he was athletic enough that he could probably dodge her swinging purse.

"It's been a while since we talked." He stepped closer to Lucy, being either incredible courageous or incredibly stupid as he ignored everyone glaring at him. "I wanted to congratulate you on your new shop, what a cool idea."

Incredibly stupid.

Lucy swallowed loudly. "Thank you." Her voice came out strong, despite how pale her face was.

"I really miss you Luce," his voice dipped to almost a whisper.

Was he trying to be seductive? Yuck. Lucy was above falling for the same jerk again.

"Maybe you shouldn't have treated her so awfully then." I snapped when Lucy seemed too surprised to say anything. He needed to go but it should be Lucy who told him off, not us.

My sharp tone seemed to jerk Lucy out of her stupor. Her gaze sought out Lucas and as soon as it did he stepped up to her side, gently resting his hand on the small of her back giving her support as he tilted his head to look down at her warmly. Oh be still my heart. A sweet feeling fluttered through my chest at the sight.

"Uh." Danny's smile faltered as he glanced from her to Lucas and back. "Luce, who is this guy?"

"She upgraded, get a clue." Madeleine looked like she might challenge him to a round of fisticuffs, except that he was almost twenty-five years younger than her and in a lot better shape. I figured we could all dogpile on him if necessary. And I had a lot of extra padding that should protect me in a fight. Wasn't that how it worked? Maybe not. At the very least I'd be hard to get off if I sat on him.

I glanced at Ro and she looked at me then flicked her gaze to Lucas with a little smirk. Yeah, we wouldn't need to worry about dealing with Danny.

"Danny, is it?" Lucas said when Lucy stayed silent. "You seem to be causing a disturbance here. Clearly all these women are uncomfortable. You should leave."

Danny looked at him, seeming to struggle to keep his glare in check, before turning his gaze back to Lucy.

"Hey." He said softly. "Why don't we go talk somewhere? I'd like to catch up with you."

She cleared her throat and squared her shoulders. "I'm dating someone Danny. I figure everything that needed to be said was when I found out you were cheating on me."

"Come one, you know it wasn't like that. It was an accident. We're all human, accidents happen in relationships."

Ro barked a short laugh while Madeleine and I scoffed. What a blighted ghost pepper liar.

Lucas gazed at him calmly, hand still resting on Lucy's back. In fact, she was subtly leaning his way.

Lucy didn't seem to know what to say and I desperately wished someone would end this tension. My chest felt tight from watching it.

Say something, Lucas.

Lucas seemed to be waiting for Lucy.

"I think you should leave. And please don't talk to me again, you made your choice and I'd rather not engage with you any further." Lucy said, her voice cracking a little.

He looked shocked. He'd been able to cajole Lucy into seeing things his way before, but not now. Now she saw him for who he really was and there was no going back from that. His eyes flicked to Lucas and then to the hand he had on her.

"Wow, you really moved on already?" He honestly seemed surprised.

I wanted to slap the look off his face. He literally was "moving on" with another woman while he was dating her. It had been over six months and she had the right to do whatever she pleased in her time anyway.

Lucy lifted her chin. "Yes, I have. goodbye." Without another word she rushed past him.

Lucas was above shoulder checking Danny as he moved past him, but Ro was not. Danny looked about as startled as I did when she bumped him, hard.

"I swear she grew up on the streets." Madeleine whispered after we cleared the gaping obstacle.

"She's ex-CIA, she can kill with a pen." It was terrible of me to tease, but it gave me an evil kind of joy to see her eyes widen at the thought. Sorry Santa, I guess I'm on the naughty list. I'll buy my own stuff.

We made it outside and I studied Lucy. She was trembling and it looked like she was about to tear up. "I'm sorry guys can you give me just a second?

I'm so sorry, I'm not usually so needlessly emotional." She glanced at Lucas as she said it.

Lucas put an arm around her shoulders. "Adrenaline." he murmured softly.

"You're allowed to be as emotional as you want." Madeleine declared.

"What's the game plan?" Ro directed the conversation back to business.

"I'm going to go to the station and run Kylie through the system." he gave us a stern look. "Do not make a move without me."

The others nodded but I pretended to be interested in the dark sky that was letting loose fat flakes of snow floating down on us, dusting our cheeks.

"Cammie." his tone held a warning.

"I don't think it hurts anything if I go chat with one of her colleagues tomorrow." I said defensively. I didn't want to give this away after everything we'd gone through to see this resolved and real justice done.

He studied me then sighed. "Why don't we go together?"

I blinked. Did he just say that? I studied him suspiciously but he didn't seem to have an ulterior motive. His calm blue eyes were honest and he met my gaze steadily.

"Okay then, I suppose I'll see you tomorrow."

"Let's meet at the construction HQ tomorrow at ten am."

"I'll be there." I shouldn't have been as excited as I was, but we were almost there, almost to the finish line.

Charles had gotten out of jail on bail, so he was with his daughter, but the threat of a long trial and prison still loomed over their heads. It had to be an oppressive weight, one a child shouldn't have to bear.

MILK, COOKIES, AND MURDER

The next day Lucas and I met at the big building that housed Woodland Construction. It used to be a mansion back in its day before being zoned for commercial use, so it had eves and a dark stained wood porch with elegant railing that formed a half moon shape from the porch down the stairs to the ground.

"I've heard you've done this before, more than a few times." he gave me the side eye as he said it, judging my reaction no doubt.

"I don't interrogate, I just talk to people." The idea of me interrogating anyone was laughable. No one would take in my middle-aged chubby form with no credentials and be intimidated.

He held the door open for me. "That's what interrogation is. It's not like in the movies at all."

"Did you come from the city?" I asked to get my mind off the nervousness tickling my stomach. I was more nervous with him at my side than I was dealing with this on my own.

"Sure did. I was ready for a change though, too many rough cases and then I got shot."

How horrifying. I glanced up at him but he didn't expound. I was not going to ask.

"I can't imagine." It had to be one of the hardest jobs out there.

We walked into the office. The receptionist saw me and gave me the same polite welcome smile, then her gaze lit on Lucas and she sat up straighter her white teeth flashing in the light like a predator about to strike.

"What can I do for you?" she asked, gaze on him, her voice far more sultry than the one she had used with me. I had one tone and I didn't know how other women managed multiple.

Irritation rose in me, he was going out with Lucy and they seem to really like each other, butt out. But it wasn't her fault that we had a small town and not a lot of younger new faces showed up.

"Yes, I wanted to speak with one of your representatives."

"Most certainly. Is there anyone in particular?"

"Not really, anyone you can recommend?"

"Uh," I interrupted, noticing that Kylie's door was closed and her office was dark. "We had been working with Ms. Treadwell, but it looks like she's not in, is there anyone who works closely with her?"

"That would be Dale. Let me take you to his office." She hurried in front of us, sashaying her hips that were well defined by her tight pencil skirt. Usually I would have thought she looked beautiful and wasn't ashamed of it, but now I was just irritated.

I glanced at Lucas, he wasn't even paying attention to her. I had a feeling that he was going to stick around, and that we were all going to really like him.

He leaned down to whisper, "you think on your feet, you should apply for a job at the station."

I was liking him less already.

"Not in a million years."

He laughed softly.

"Dale, someone here to see you. It sounds like they've been working with Kylie on a few things and wanted to talk with you."

Dale was a stout, balding man with a friendly smile and warm voice. "Come on in." He shook our hands as we entered. "Have a seat."

The receptionist lingered in the doorway, eyes continuing to be drawn back to Lucas. "Is there anything I can get you? Coffee, tea?" Someone to go on a date with? I could see it in her eyes.

Dale looked at us.

"No thank you." Lucas said firmly.

I shook my head but she wasn't even paying attention to me.

She looked disappointed but mustered a smile, "let me know if you need anything." she left.

"What can I do for you both?" He smiled, waving between us, "I can tell you're mom and son."

MILK, COOKIES, AND MURDER

I choked, coughing hard.

Lucas reached over and patted my back. "There, there, mom. I keep telling you that I look more like you than dad."

I was going to throttle the man. A son in his thirties indeed. I fumed silently.

He suppressed a smile and turned his full attention to Dale. "I actually have a few questions about your colleague, Kylie Treadwell."

Dale's brow wrinkled in confusion but he nodded.

"What can you tell me about her relationship with Darwin Lodus?"

His eyebrows flew up. "Oh. Well." he glanced around as if trying to find the right words.

"There's no judgment, no matter what you say. I don't believe in saying nice things about the dead if they weren't good people when they were alive."

He looked relieved at Lucas's assurance. "Darwin was good at his job, good with the clients. But he was hard to work with. He always had to be the smartest man in the room, and he always seemed to get his way even when he didn't do the most work and he always acted shifty. I can't say I ever had any problems with him, but he took credit for work that I knew was Kylie's, and ended up with the promotion she should have had." His look was condemning. I understood the sentiment.

"Did they ever argue in front of you?"

He thought about it then shook his head. "He teased her an awful lot, said things that were borderline harassment if you ask me, but she never said anything and I know that Jack would have dealt with it if she'd complained to him."

That sounded to me like the recipe for a pressure cooker about to burst. Lucas didn't betray any of his thoughts on his face so I tried to keep as neutral as possible as well. I wasn't a good actor though, I probably looked like I was in pain.

We gathered more information about her, including that she went to a boxing gym. That got a "hmm" from Lucas.

After conversing with him for a few more minutes we both thanked him and head it out.

"Why was the boxing gym of such interest to you?" I asked.

"Slamming a ice pick far enough into someone's chest to kill them would take some strength."

I'd gotten a C minus in a human biology college class many years ago and I still had no interest in knowing about the human body, much less the strength needed to end someone's life with a weapon.

"Just so we're on the same page, you believe she did it, right?" I said as we stopped by our vehicles.

He studied me. He was beginning to do that a lot, and it made me self-conscious.

"I cannot just say that she did it, Cammie. There is a lot more that needs to be in place. Evidence, or a confession, preferably both."

I thought of something. "The ice pick didn't have any prints?" I doubted it, giving that everyone was wearing mittens or gloves, but it would have been much more convenient.

"We never found the murder weapon."

My brows furrowed. "You searched the area?"

He gave me a look that said he didn't appreciate me implying that he couldn't do his job. I waved my hands in surrender. "Okay, okay. I just needed to double check for my own sanity."

Where could she have left the murder weapon?

"Cammie" Lucas said warily. "We searched four blocks in each direction and didn't find anything."

"Interesting." I murmured, more to myself than to him as my mind raced over the possibilities.

"Do not do anything without me. I'm going to see if that background came in on her." He said sternly.

Good thing I wasn't easily intimidated by man young enough people assumed he was my son. I would be pained by that comment forever.

"I'll see you later."

Chapter 18

Lucas and I both went back to our day and my mind kept going over and over the places Kylie could have the murder weapon. She'd clearly taken it with her when she left the scene. Wait, didn't gyms have lockers? She wouldn't have thought to hide it in there, would she?

It wouldn't hurt to check it out.

As I was closing up the Cultural Arts Center for the day, Lucy texted me.

Lucy: *anything new? anything I can do to help? I talked to Charles to see if there is any information he could provide that might be helpful, but there isn't anything.*

I typed back quickly: *I have an idea where she might have hidden the murder weapon. I'm going there now.*

Lucy: *WAIT! Don't go by yourself.*

Me: *don't worry, It might not be anything and she won't suspect a thing. She's probably not even there.*

Lucy: *where?*

I got in my car, ignoring her for the moment.

Lucy: *PLEASE. So I don't worry?*

Me: *Her boxing gym. I think it might be in a locker.*

Hopefully she hadn't put it in the dumpster because it would have been collected and taken to the dump by now and we'd be out of luck.

Lucy didn't say anything else so I put Buttercup in gear and drove over to the boxing gym. I pulled into the nearly emptying parking lot. That was a good sign, I would be able to get in and nose around without too many eyes on me. If anyone asked I would just say that I'm thinking about taking up boxing to get into shape. The idea horrified me but they didn't have to know that.

The gym smelled like others I'd been in, rubber, sweat, cleaning reagents. There were weight racks on one wall, a couple of ellipticals and a couple of treadmills on the well diagonal to it, and a big wide open space covered in mats. It had punching bags to one side. This must be where they trained. It looked intimidating.

There were a couple of men, but they were occupied with the weights they had and talking about some kind of powder. One was holding up a bottle of green sludge. Ro should have come, she would fit right in.

I hurried toward the back, where an opening beckoned me further. It must lead to the changing rooms. I nearly ran into the men's area before realizing my mistake and turning on my heel. I did not need to make this the most embarrassing day of my life.

There were three showers behind frosted glass doors, a couple of sinks and bathroom stalls, and further in was a locker room. There were no names, and the ones that would prove to have something in them were locked of course. Clearly I hadn't thought this through. I needed to get Ro, she could pick any lock. Even with prodding she wouldn't say what she'd done in the CIA to require her to pick locks, but my imagination was vivid. She would probably laugh at some of the scenarios that I'd came up with.

I hurried back out toward the main room, freezing when I heard a familiar voice.

"...Yeah, I've been upping the weights lately." Kylie said, most likely talking to the two men who had been by the weight racks.

I peeked around the corner. She had dumped her duffel bag next to the water fountain on the wall. There was a bulge in a small, zippered pocket on the side of the black bag.

I tried to stroll as casually as possible, not making any sudden movements that would draw their eyes, getting closer to the bag.

I kept an eye on her, but she was deep in conversation with the two men. Were they seriously still talking about the green powder?

Closer, closer. There. I bent down a little, keeping her in the peripheral of my vision while I insanely slipped the zipper open. The sound was deafening and I flinched. No one noticed me. Sure enough, there were keys in the pocket. I gripped them and slipped them out. She started to turn, I didn't have time to zip up the bag. I stood quickly and slammed the water fountain button, causing a spurt to shoot high up and spatter on my blouse. Oh goodie.

"Cammie?" Kylie called, coming closer.

I turned, pretending to be surprised. "Oh hi. How are you? I didn't realize you came to this gym." my voice cracked even as I struggled to calm my thundering heart. Thievery was wrong and I was going to have to spend the next several nights doing good things to make this up to my conscience.

"Yeah," she looked at me curiously. "Are you thinking of coming?"

"Uh," I glanced around, "honestly no. But I told my doctor I would try to find a gym to work out at during the cold winter months when I can't walk outside as much." At least I didn't have to lie again.

She smiled, maybe sensing that I was telling the truth. "You really should think about it, it's a great sport and total body fitness."

"I'll do that. I should go check out the rest of the place now." I backed away from her. I noticed the guys were packing up.

"Okay. See you." Her brows were lowered, as if she thought I was odd and was confused.

Little did she know she was not the only one.

I forced myself to walk calmly to the back area where I promptly clutched my chest. My doctor always said it was good that I kept my stress so low, I wonder what she'd say now? Best not to think about it.

I tried a few different padlocks, with a few different keys. On my fifth try I struck gold. It was a heavy duty lock securing the metal door and I popped it off.

There was nothing inside except for a single shirt. It was thrown in in a messy way, not folded. Compelled, I reached in and picked it up. I had thought it was a possibility, but the fact that I actually found the murder weapon shocked me to silence. I needed to tell Lucas about this, right away. I replaced the shirt, quietly closed the door and snapped the lock back into place, wincing at the loud noise it made, echoing through the room.

I tried to calm my thrashing pulse before going out back out to the main room. Surely I wasn't the only one who could hear it.

Kylie was now the only person there. She had earbuds in and was running on the treadmill. I scurried over to her bag, dropped the keys in it and zipped it closed before heading toward the door as fast as I could without running.

Outside I breathed in the bitterly cold air with relief. I made it.

A strong hand clamped around my bicep and I yelped, swinging my hand around to smack.

My eyes opened wide.

Lucas glanced down where my hand has smacked his chest. Or rather, his officer vest. He twitched an eyebrow, "you do know that it's illegal to assault an officer right?"

I gasped. "You surprised me! I thought it was self-defense. I really didn't mean to, are you hurt?" I blubbered and patted the spot where I'd smacked him.

He began to laugh, a rich sound that reverberated warmly from his chest, and I realized that he was making fun of me.

I opened my mouth to inform him that we didn't have time to doddle, but Lucy drove up, practically skidding into a parking spot. She hurried over to us.

"Oh Cammie thank goodness. Thank you, Lucas. You can't go around scaring me like that!"

I held my hand up to stave off further fussing. "You can yell at me later, the murder weapon is in Kylie's locker."

Lucy gaped at me while Lucas widened his eyes, clearly surprised that I'd found anything.

"I don't have probable cause for that locker besides the fact that you broke in. That doesn't look good in court." he said.

I didn't know what to say, it was right there why couldn't he take it and prove she was the murderer?

His eyes turned somber. "Cammie, you said you wouldn't do anything without me. You're lucky Lucy called me."

"No I didn't, and yes I am." He may have ordered me not to do anything without him, but I had not agreed to it.

"I'm going to go in there and try to get her to open that locker." he said, turning toward the door.

"Wait." I put a hand on his arm, stilling him. "I should go in and talk to her alone, see if she'll slip up and say anything." I took a breath. "If it really would be so bad that I am the one who told you about the locker, we should try to get more out of her first."

Lucas frowned. "We need to be careful, if she truly killed him she might not hesitate to hurt you should you feel like a threat to her."

"I'll keep my distance and if anything happens you can come rescue me."

He looked like he was going to argue so before he could say anything I hurried forward.

Back in the building I called her name, "Kylie."

She turned from the weight rack to look at me. Was it my imagination or was that unease that flashed across her face? Maybe it was my own assumptions at work causing me to see something that wasn't there.

"Liked it so much that you're back so soon?" She asked with a smile that didn't reach her eyes.

"Actually, after seeing you I realize you might be able to help me so I came to talk to you. I feel like you could be a vital help. I've been helping Charles and Jenny Cameron out and I've been looking into who really could have killed Darwing."

Her eyes widened marginally. "Really? Isn't that the police's job?"

"I don't like to leave things to chance so I've been trying to track all possible leads in case they missed something." I could feel Lucas's glare through the wall.

"Okay," she said slowly, "what info do you need from me?"

"Well, given that you worked with him, I feel like you know him better than most of the people I talk to."

She snorted. "There wasn't much to know."

"But he was such a tyrant, right?" Come on, come on tell me how awful he was and that you finally snapped.

"He was." she didn't offer anything more.

I was losing her.

"I heard someone say that you did it to get the promotion." It was a desperate gamble on my part to be so obvious.

She froze, staring at me. She quickly snapped out of it and flashed an uneasy smile, "who said that?"

"Um, it was just something I heard."

I hadn't noticed it, but now my attention caught on the fact that she had moved so that she was closer to the door and I had taken a few steps further into the vacant gym.

Ghost Peppers.

"I'm sure the police will understand, and you will get a good lawyer." I said, trying to sound soothing instead of hysterical.

"Is that why you stole my keys?"

My blood turned to ice in my veins. "Keys?" I squeaked.

"You left the zipper open. I never leave the zipper open." she narrowed her eyes at me, locking on like she was a predator and I was her prey. "Did you find it?"

I nodded, unable to get past the fearful lump in my throat. This hadn't been such a good idea.

In one smooth move she stepped up to the door slammed it closed and locked it. There went my rescue.

"You're a nice lady, you should have kept your nose out of it. I really feel bad about this." she said. "But I've worked too hard in my life for this to keep me down."

I tried to keep distance between us, even as she stalked toward me. Not good, not good.

"Kylie we can talk about this. They can understand one murder, but another one? They won't go on as easy on you for the second one."

"I'm never going to jail over this." she said through gritted teeth.

She rushed forward and I tried to dodge out of the way. I managed to, partly. Her knuckles grazed across my cheek, sending a throb through my face. I landed on my backside.

I scooted backwards, unable to get to my feet fast enough, and looked desperately for help. My gaze landed on a steel bar that was used to put round weights on, and something clicked. I grabbed it. In one swift motion throwing all of the weight I possibly could behind it, I sent it flying her way. It smacked her in the forehead and I winced at the sound. I had meant for it to hit her shoulder. She dropped, hard.

At the same time, Lucas kicked through the door.

"Cammie!" Lucy raced over to me and fell to her knees, wrapping her arms around me.

"I'm fine, I'm fine. I have a lot of padding where I landed." I assured her, giving her a quick hug in return and then trying, unsuccessfully, to get her to loosen her hold on me.

With cuffs on a dazed Kylie and the ambulance and police called Lucas came over and crouched by me. He carefully checked where she'd grazed me. "It's going to be sore for a week, maybe two, but I don't think it's broken. As angry as I am at you," he started and I winced, "that was pretty good presence of mind. What made you do it?"

"In the twelfth and thirteenth centuries jousting was fairly popular. A couple years ago I went to a competition that honored the sport and when I saw the metal bar it seemed like a decent way to get her to stop chasing me."

His eyes crinkled at his he smiled at me. "You're one crazy woman, you know that?"

"Lucas!" Lucy gasped.

I grinned, "you sure you want to get dragged further into the crazy?"

He glanced at Lucy and then back at me. "I think it's worth it." he sobered. "But you," he gave me a distinct look, "no more running off to do nonsense like this. This is the police's job and you need to be done with all of this now."

I didn't mention that the police hadn't done their job and that was why I got involved in the first place, I was just too relieved to be done with it all. I would be happy to get back to my normal, boring days.

I had just one more thing to resolve before Christmas.

Chapter 19

Lucy's grand opening was twelve days before Christmas, which I thought was delightful. I'd suggested that she play the twelve days of Christmas song over and over again but she nixed that right away. Actually, she said that was a great idea and she would certainly put that on her list. The music playing tonight was anything but.

As White Christmas, Rockin' Around the Christmas Tree, and others, a mix of classic and modern songs played, people chatted, nibbled on treats and looked through the books and unique items she had lined up beautifully for sale. The place was packed. She had a discount for anyone coming to the grand opening, and books were flying off the shelves. So were the unique bookmarks, and even some pictures that she'd had an artist paint, the back of a woman sitting in a tree swing in summer, reading a book. I would know, I'd bought one.

A beaming Jenny stuck to her dad's side as he talked to various people. His face was lit up with new life and purpose and he'd said that he was going to try to give back more and create a scholarship for kids who demonstrated decent high school standing and had a parent was in jail. Their parents decisions weren't their fault and he'd been terrified about what would happen to his daughter without him to provide.

Ro sidled up to me. "You've been jumping every time the door opens. Is there a reason there'd be a hit out on you or something?"

I chuckled, "No, I'm waiting for someone. I will never be important enough to warrant a hit from anyone, though the chief might want to order one because of how annoying he finds me." When the reporter had pressed he had said that I had done a fine job in assisting them, but that people should leave the police work to the police and stay busy going about their own lives.

Her eyebrows rose and curiosity sparked in her eyes. "So Lucy isn't the only one Santa gifted with a man?"

"Ugh." I sent a glare her way before quickly casting my gaze back to the door. "My request to Santa was to keep trouble *out* of my life."

"Fair enough."

I wanted to tell her what was going on, but it was private and not mine to share.

The door opened and a woman in her early sixties walked in. She had recognizable features and I knew instantly it was her. Hurrying forward I greeted her.

"Ariadne, right?"

"Yes. Cammie?"

"That's me." We shook hands. "I cannot thank you enough for coming."

"No." She gripped my hand strongly. "It's I who should be thanking you."

"I believe this is yours." I handed her the music box which I've been clutching protectively all night and she took it carefully, tenderly running her finger over the etching. "Ready to meet him?"

She looked nervous but squared her shoulders. "Whatever happens, this has been needed for decades."

I led her across the room to where Victor was sitting on the couch, watching children play with a melancholic expression.

"Victor. I'd like to introduce someone to you."

He glanced up and stood quickly. They locked eyes and it was as if time stopped. My heart was in my throat and I couldn't even introduce them.

"Ariadne?" He whispered.

Her eyes filled with tears and one snuck down her cheek. "It's me, dad."

"My baby." Shock froze his face.

I backed away, my heart tearing into a thousand pieces and then mending as I watched them reunited at last after such a cruel twist of fate was dealt. I turned and hurried to where the ladies were standing together, looking over at the reunion.

"What did you do?"

"It turns out that Victor's wife took their daughter and left without saying a word nearly fifty years ago."

"What?" They exclaimed.

"She was from a wealthy family but fell in love with Victor and married him only to end up unhappy with their economic conditions despite him working eighteen hour days to bring in enough money to make her happy. One December he came home to her and their daughter's things cleared out. He spent all his savings and everything he made trying to find them, but he never could track them down."

Lucy had tears in her eyes and she sniffled. "That's awful."

"Usually stories like that don't get a happy ending." Ro smiled the softest smile I think I'd ever seen on her face. Who was the sap now? Still me, but Ro was in that category now too and I would find a way to reminder her of it at some point.

"How did you know?" Lucy asked.

"The initials, VT. And then in the little drawer of the box there was a paper with Ariadne's name on it. After digging through a lot of Ariadne's living in the U.S. I just had the thought that maybe I should use Victor's last name because of the initials. It was sheer luck."

"It was you being thorough and refusing to give up." Ro said.

"Cammie." Madeleine whispered. I glanced at her and she nodded toward one of the shelves. I followed her gaze.

The ghost stood there, looking on at the woman and her dad as where they sat on the couch, hands clasped together and talking animatedly. Then he vanished.

"Wow." Lucy breathed.

"And that my beautiful friends, is how you get rid of a ghost." I smiled.

Now the ghost, and Victor and Ariadne, had found peace.

Chapter 20

Christmas eve arrived in no time and found me wrapping gifts in wrapping paper that I felt embodied the person it was for the most. Gavin had gifts wrapped in green paper with dancing elves and black paper with swirling gold Christmas trees and snowflakes. Lucy had green paper patterned with adorable snowmen. Madeleine had red paper with Christmas foliage. Ro got dark green with realistic mountains and fir trees.

Outside the wind whipped, causing the house to creak even as I enjoyed the roaring faux fireplace, padding around in my fluffy slippers as I got everything ready for dinner. Gavin was already at the house, napping because he was recovering from a cold, and the ladies would show up soon.

Think of the devil. Gavin wandered in, his hair, dark with red on the spiked ends, was sticking in more directions than when he had arrived this morning.

"Ooh." He snagged a petite beef wellington off the tiered tray.

I waved my wooden spoon at him threateningly.

He held his palms up in surrender, but not before he popped it into his mouth and moaned at the taste. "I need more."

"You'll get more when dinner is served here in about half an hour."

He took the stack of Christmas plates and silverware I had set out to the table, laying them out along with the red cloth napkins that were dusted with white snowflakes.

Someone knocked gently on the door, then pushed it open because I'd told everyone to just come in.

"Hiiii!" Lucy was sure happy lately.

I smiled. "Hi Lucy."

"Hello, hello." Gavin greeted, going over to give her a squeeze after she placed her dish on the countertop.

"Get those snowy boots out of my kitchen." I said mildly.

"Sorry, sorry!" She tried to tiptoe back to the entry but one did not tiptoe in bulky winter boots and all she managed to do was squeak them against the floor and knock more snow off.

"How deep is it?" I attacked the snow with a paper towel before anyone could go sliding across the floor and end up in a Christmas cast.

"Around four inches right now. It keeps coming though."

And the wind was picking up.

"Gavin, do you have a weather reader on your phone?"

"Sure do."

"What does it say for tonight?"

"The weather app says that the snow isn't supposed to stop until tomorrow mid-morning, accumulation is between four to seven inches. And the wind is picking up."

We were headed into a blizzard. It hadn't said that two days ago when I checked.

Suddenly Ro and Madeline were in with us, and as I looked around the room filled with my loved ones, I didn't care about the weather or anything else for that matter.

We bustled about, managing not to smack into each other in my small cottage as we set the table. They had all brought something and all were wearing the fluffy slippers that I had gotten for them as they wandered around my house.

I tapped Madeleine on the arm and stepped into the hallway. She followed.

"How were things at home?" I had been surprised when Madeleine said she could make it since she was the only one with family in town.

She looked more relaxed than she had in a while. "Lawrence and I had a good talk a few days ago. They're still being stressful and dogmatic, but we're presenting a united front." she smiled. "Lawrence even defended me when they fussed because I was coming over here for Christmas Eve dinner. Usually he's the peacekeeper and just changes the subject to something else, but he actually stood up to them. Besides, I ordered a whole dinner from a restaurant for them and Lawrence and I usually celebrate Christmas day instead of Christmas Eve, so I'll be there with them then."

I gave her a quick hug. "I'm glad."

Dinner lasted almost two hours with us all chatting, Lucy telling us all about her dates with Lucas, Ro giving up a rare story of when she was in the CIA overseas staking out an undisclosed location during Christmas, and Gavin sharing his most outrageous tales from the salon.

By the time the plates were cleared the house trembled from the power of the whipping wind. Gavin clicked on the porch light and looked out the window.

"I don't think anyone's going home tonight." he said.

Ro angled next to him and peered out. "The lower vehicles would get stuck right away." she said.

"I have all-wheel drive." Madeleine said. She traded places with Gavin at the window. "On second thought, all-wheel drive doesn't help when you can't see more than two feet in front of you."

I headed down the hallway to the linen closet and grabbed a bin, carrying it into the living room. I popped the top off and set it to the side. "All sorts of cozy blankets in here, pick your favorite."

I turned Christmas music up and we enjoyed it with the dim lights with the flickering fire while the storm raged outside. Madeleine let her husband know and he said he just wanted her to be safe.

We all laughed as a more enthusiastic Christmas song pumped out and Gavin danced around, wiggling his bum and twirling like a ballerina.

It got late and we all started to settle down, picking our favorite chairs in the living room.

"Should we watch The Bishop's Wife?" lucy suggested.

Who could say no to Cary Grant?

"Yes, let's do that." I grabbed the remote.

She curled up on the couch and put her head on the pillow in my lap. I fixed the blanket around her small form. She smiled sleepily.

"I was upset about my family being gone on that cruise, but I love you all and I'm so happy that I'm here. It was worth it." she murmured.

"We love you too." Madeleine said.

"Remember that we said it before Lucas. We count first." Ro said, eliciting a laugh from us.

As peaceful quiet blanketed the room I looked around and found that my heart was full. Justice had been served in our town, a daughter and her father had been reunited after nearly 50 years, and the people who mattered to me the most were safe and happy around me.

The End? Hardly!

Dive into summer at Whispering Lake where a death is not as it looks and it turns out ghosts aren't as benevolent as they thought.

Get the special pre-order price on book 3, Canoeing into Chaos.

Releasing 1/17/25

Whispering Lake Paranormal Cozy Murder Mysteries

Ghost at the Garden Gate
Milk, Cookies, and Murder
Canoeing into Chaos

About the Author

Misty is the intrepid investigator of murders and paranormal mysteries, a lover of hot cider on snowy days and stories where the good guys(and gals!) always win. Misty exists only on paper. She is the pseudonym of a woman whose favorite part of the day is after work when she can sit down and craft mysteries she hopes you will love.